SHROUD₃
From
Shroud Publishing LLC

You are holding a limited edition small press publication in your hands. This book is a result of hard work and creative effort. Enjoy it and celebrate the possibility of all things.

Designed and Printed in the USA

**SP
Shroud Publishing**

www.shroudmagazine.com

First Edition
First Printing July 15, 2008
Copyright 2008 Shroud Publishing
All Rights Reserved

The individual copyrights of the respective authors herein reverted back to the original copyright holder upon publication.

Cover Art by Bart Willard
http://www.bartwillard.com

ISBN: 978-0-9801870-6-9

Shroud Publishing LLC
121 Mason Rd.
Milton, NH 03851
www.shroudmagazine.com

The Bram Stoker Award-nominated novella *"Mama's Boy"* is the cornerstone of this 14-story collection from author Fran Friel and Apex Publications. From mother and son to broader family ties, Friel explores the bonds of human connection into every dark turn.

"Scary stories that are not soon forgotten. And from such a nice person. Highly recommended."
– Gene O'Neill, Author of *COLLECTED TALES OF THE BAJA EXPRESS* and *THE CONFESSIONS OF ST. ZACH*

ISBN:
TPB 978-0-9816390-8-6
HC 978-0-9816390-7-9

Brotherly love is a deadly seduction, beauty a dangerous game. Come worship in the brutal temple of Orgy of Souls. Your faith will never be the same again.

A new novella from horror masters Wrath James White and Maurice Broaddus.

"Broaddus and White are an unlikely pairing of talents that works astonishingly well. *Orgy of Souls* is a powerful, innovative work of fiction and one I recommend wholeheartedly. A damned fine read!"
– James A. Moore, author of *DEEPER* and *CHERRY HILL*

ISBN:
TPB 978-0-9816390-4-8
Available in limited hardcover, signed. Only 350 copies printed.

APEX PUBLICATIONS
www.ApexBookCompany.com

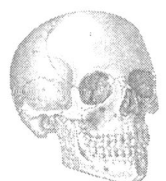
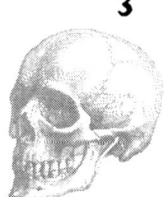

Shroud 3, Summer 2008

SHROUD₃

The Journal of Dark Fiction and Art

Shroud 3
Summer 2008

Publisher
Shroud Publishing LLC

Editor
Timothy P. Deal

Assistant Editor
Robert Canipe

Marketing
Jennifer N. Deal

Layout and Design
Dale Mythito

Contributing Editors
I.E. Lester
Shawn Oetzel
Steve Vernon

Contributing Artists
Bart Willard

Cover Art
Bart Willard

ISSN
1940-7025

Copyright (c) 2007 by Shroud Publishing LLC. Individual works are copyright (c) 2007 by their respective creators. All rights reserved.

Fiction

THEY HAD GOAT HEADS, D. Harlan Wilson	6
ON THE BRINK OF EXTINCTION, Shaun Jeffrey	12
SIDE EFFECTS WILL OCCUR, Sheldon S. Higdon	17
NOVEL SINCERE, Jeffrey Jewett	22
BLUE MOON FEVER, Tina L. Jens	27
SHADOWS IN THE SNOW, Phil Kuhlman	36
A MUSEUM PIECE, Ken Goldman	40
THE FOWLER'S DAUGHTER, Michele Muenzler	45
OLD SCHOOL TIES, Joseph D'Lacey	50
ANGEL, RAPE WHEELCHAIR, Robert Davies	56
THE JESUS ORCHID, JG Faherty	65
SCORNED, Joseph McGee	86
MYSPACE FLASH FICTION CONTEST #2	89

Nonfiction

THE HEARTLESS DUC D'ANVILLE, Steve Vernon	6
MICHAEL MARSHALL SMITH, interview by Marie O'Regan	32
WILLIAM JONES, interview by Jeff Edwards	59
THE BLACK DOG, Kurt Bachard	85
THE AMAZING ART OF BART WILLARD, Tim Deal	97

Books

HEBREW PUNK by Lavi Tidhar	75
POE, A LIFE CUT SHORT by Peter Ackroyd	76
AGNES HAHN by Richard Satterlie	76
OLD FLAMES by Jack Ketchum	77
SAINT GERMAIN: MEMOIRS by Chelsea Q. Yarbro	79

Film

THE MOTHER of TEARS, by Tim Deal	95

Extras

PUZZLED: Horror Novel Crossword, I.E. Lester	101
SOLUTION	103

MISSIVES

Shroud was happy to receive these reactions to the availability of our second issue. We'd really appreciate hearing from you as well. Please email us at editor@shroudmagazine.com. We would sincerely love to hear your ideas for making Shroud better. You can also join our forum at www.shroudmagazine.com. Thank you!

Dear Tim,

Thank you so much for the wondrous copy of Shroud I'm delighted and honoured to be in there and the whole mag is terrific. Terrific work.

Warmest wishes,

Ken Bruen

Dear Tim,

Magazine looks incredible! Gorgeous cover, love the layout and the perfect-binding. Sweet! hope folks are digging the Pic & Bruen story.

Best,

Tom Piccirilli

Dearest one

I know this mail will come as a surprise to you. I have a proposal for you to this project however is not mandatory nor will I in any manner compel you to honor against your will, Your profile pushed me to send you this mail, I am Master Newman Roberts, I am 22 years old and the only Son of my late parents Dr. and Mrs. Roberts Didie. My father was a highly reputable farmer (a cocoa merchant) in cote d' ivories during his days.

It is sad to say that he was poisoned and passed away mysteriously in France during one of his business trips abroad on 12th. May 2007.Though his sudden death was linked or rather suspected to have been masterminded by my uncle who traveled with him at that
time. But God knows the truth! My mother died when I was just 4 years old, and since then my father took me so special.

Before he made the trip to France that lead to my misfortune (his death) He called me and explained to me the reason why he will make this trip and also told me that he deposited a fund that contain US$ 12.5000000 (Thelve Million Five Hundred Thousand Dollars) in a Bank there in Abidjan Ivory Coast and that this money is for an investment purpose overseas.

He gave me the certificate that he used for the deposit of the fund and other vital documents of his asset, after his death I went to the Bank and establish
ownership of the fund. Now I need your assistance to move this fund to your country for investment as that has been my late father's aim before his death. Now permit me to ask these few questions: -

Can you honestly help me receive the said fund in your country ?
Thanks for your Understanding,

Master Newman Roberts

- - - - - - - - - - - -

> We'd love to hear from you!
> Send your ideas, suggestions, criticism and praise to editor@ shroudmagazine.com

Shroud 3   The Journal of Dark Fiction and Art

From The Editor:
The Joy of Fear
And the Gnashing of Teeth
Tim Deal

Welcome to the long-awaited Shroud 3. I appreciate your patience as we struggled to wrangle all of this wonderful content into a hundred or so pages. I am going to keep this introduction short because the printer is waiting for these files so that they can expedite the print run. We have an outstanding lineup of veteran authors alongside of some stimulating new voices in the genre. I know you are going to enjoy every heaping helping of Shroud in this volume because I have. Shroud is going strong with orders and submissions, anthologies, and novellas and we hope that our reputation as a quality publisher continues unabated. Please trust that you should not have to wait as long for Shroud 4 to come out as we are hoping to streamline this process as much as possible. Once again, thank you all for your support and please tell your friends about Shroud!

Sheldon S. Higdon, Tim Deal, Christa M. Miller

Shroud 3   The Journal of Dark Fiction and Art

Shroud Flash Fiction
THEY HAD GOAT HEADS
D. HARLAN WILSON

They had goat heads . . .

I could see down the hallway from the bed. It stretched two miles into the forest. My mother served me a bowl of vegetable soup. The door was open. I wanted to close it.

The TV turned on. A goat walked back and forth across the screen. Then a tall, thin man entered the picture and slaughtered the goat with an axe. The camera zoomed into the man's face. He gazed down at the carcass, eyes wide with terror, mouth slowly opening into a chemical scream . . .

The TV turned off. A brick crashed through the window. There was a note tied to it. I picked it up and read the note.

"They have goat heads," it read. I looked out the window. An astronaut in a bubble helmet and orange spacesuit waved at me, then boarded his shuttle. Liftoff. The motel shook. The shuttle rose like a flag, gaining speed and altitude until it disappeared into the clouds.

Thunder. The clouds flashed, flickered . . . The shuttle fell out of the sky, smoldering . . . It crashed onto its launch pad and burst into flames. The motel shook . . .

A door creaked open and the astronaut climbed out. He staggered into a tree and bounced backwards. He looked at the wreckage. He looked at me and took off his bubble helmet. He had a goat head.

I drew the curtain. Somebody in the ceiling had attached marionette strings to my mother's joints. They had also stapled her lips onto her cheeks. Her teeth were two rows of golf tees. She made desperate sucking noises as the puppeteer compelled her to dust the room and vacuum the carpet.

I heard bleating in the hallway. I told my mother I would be right back.

I shut the door behind me. For two miles, all of the doors were closed, and I didn't see anyone except a meter maid who tried to take my pulse with a lightning rod. Then I saw an open door. Room 3,401D. I heard cheering inside.

I went inside. They wanted to play basketball in the boxing ring. Hoops loomed over the ring's turnbuckles. The coaches screamed at each other. The referees ran back and forth and bounced off the ropes, testing their resilience. The players held hands and prayed. They all had goat heads.

I noticed my old college roommate in the audience. He was sitting next to my ex-girlfriend, making out with her. He pretended not to see me . . . I walked up two flights of bleachers and sat by myself.

A referee blew a whistle. Tipoff. . .

My mother lumbered into 3,401D. The puppeteer maneuvered her into the boxing ring, scaring away the dramatis personae. A microphone descended from the ceiling on a thin length of cord and she gurgled into it.

They played the bagpipes . . . I stood and walked downstairs and left 3,401D. The crowd broke into hysterics as I shut the door . . . and went back to my room . . .

I got lost. I found the lobby. A motel clerk asked to see my room key. I didn't have it. He tried to have me arrested. I ran away. I got lost . . .

Time lapse of bellhops and concierges and janitors racing up and down the hallways . . . silhouette of the motel set against a blazing horizon. I hadn't taken a nap since infancy. All I wanted was a nap.

I crawled the rest of the way . . .

My mother was sleeping in my bed. She looked like a dead seal . . . No sign of the puppeteer, and the marionette strings were gone. Open wounds covered her body where the strings had been ripped free. And her lips had been cut off . . . I shook her awake and asked her to leave. She made a deflating sound.

Through the window I saw them, thousands of them, tying notes to bricks . . .

◇◇◇◇◇

D. Harlan Wilson is the author of three collections of short fiction and a science fiction novel, **Dr. Identity** *(2007), the first installment of the "Scikungfi" trilogy, which will be followed by Codename Prage (2009) and The Kyoto Man (2010). His stories and essays have appeared in magazines, journals and anthologies throughout the world in several languages. He is the editor-in-chief of The Dream People (www.dreampeople.org). For more information, visit www.dharlanwilson.com.*

HAUNTINGS, FREAKS AND MYSTERIES

THE HEARTLESS DUC D'ANVILLE

BY STEVE VERNON

Author's note: Shroud Magazine asked me to write a column on real world "haunts", based on my work as a collector of ghost stories. I felt I ought to start off with something from my stomping grounds – Halifax, Nova Scotia.

The Heartless Duc D'Anville

75,000 years ago a pack of glaciers dragged their feet across Nova Scotia, gouging out a harbour and leaving behind a pimple of an island that came to be called George's Island. For the last 150 years there have been reports of a ghost dressed in the uniform of an 18th Century French Admiral – Duc D'Anville.

This is his story.

In 1746 a French armada of 65 ships sailed from Rochelle under the command of Admiral Jean-Batiste, De Roye de la Rochefoucauld, otherwise known as Duc D'Anville. The fleet was to land in Halifax Harbour, join up with a previously organized force and take Nova Scotia from the British.

However, two storms, bad water, spoiled food and an outbreak of typhus ruined those plans. By the time they reached Halifax the Mi'kmaq and French forces that were to have met them had dispersed. The sailors landed on George's Island, believing it to be their safest refuge. They

Two hundred years of military activity - George's Island is a hotbed of tales of executions, exiles, treasure and secret tunnels and above all else the ghost of Duc D'Anville.

built a makeshift hospital from broken masts and tattered sails. Their first patient was Duc D'Anville. He keeled over during a morning inspection. Some said it was poison but a ship's surgeon declared it apoplexy – which back then was a fancy way of saying "Beats me, the guy just dropped down dead."

They cut D'Anville's heart out and sealed it in wax in a small tin bucket. The wax-covered heart was presented to D'Anville's wife and three children, back in France. The rest of D'Anville was hastily buried on George's Island. D'Anville's second-in-command, a clumsy fellow named Vice-Admiral d'Estournelle, discouraged by the whole situation, threw himself on his sword, attempting suicide. He messed that up and lived.

The armada sailed back to France in October. Over 1800 sailors and soldiers were lost to that foolish enterprise. In 1749, shortly after the British settled in Halifax, a French warship, Le Grande Saint Esprit, sailed into the harbour and dug up D'Anville's remains. They transported his coffin to Louisburg, the fort he'd come to eventually conquer, which was ceded to the French two years following D'Anville's death. D'Anvilled was re-buried with full military honours at the foot of the high altar in the Louisburg chapel.

Since D'Anville's death there have been dozens of documented sightings of a mysterious figure in Napoleonic dress who walks from George's Island and around the Harbour, his head bowed down beneath the weight of some monstrous shame. Folks who know claim that this figure is none other than the spectre of Duc D'Anville. Perhaps he's looking for his wife, perhaps he looking for his heart, perhaps he's merely looking for his way back home.

◇◇◇◇◇

Steve Vernon is Halifax, Nova Sco-

tia's hardest working horror writer. He has been collecting and writing ghost stories and weird tales for a very long time. His ghost story collections - **Haunted Harbours: Ghost Stories from Old Nova Scotia and Wicked Woods: Ghost Stories from Old New Brunswick** are available at Amazon, Barnes & Noble, Chapters/Indigo and directly from the publisher Nimbus Publishing.

Shroud Publishing presents

Northern Haunts
100 Terrifying New England Tales

AVAILABLE NOW AS LOW AS $19.99!

Edited by
TIM DEAL

100 terrifying New England tales for reading or retelling around the campfire. Completely original stories of the American old country from some of today's masters of modern horror. A collection unlike any published before-a resource and a source of hours of thrilling entertainment. A dark Yankee treasure!

ORDER AT WWW.SHROUDMAGAZINE.COM

GET GRUESOME!

Special Signed & Numbered Limited Edition of Gregory Lamberson's Novel JOHNNY GRUESOME from Bad Moon Books
Featuring an Introduction by Jeff Strand and Six Full Color Illustrations by Zach McCain

"Bold and trashy in all the right ways, Johnny Gruesome is a book (and a villain) you won't soon forget."
-- *Lee Thomas, author of PARISH DAMNED and THE DUST of WONDERLAND*

"Johnny Gruesome has a frightening sense of detail that makes it all the more horrific -- it's a gruesome ride that you can't stop reading." -- *Gunnar Hansen, Leatherface*

ALSO AVAILABLE

The 'GRUESOME' Rock CD By Giasone and Marcy Italiano!
The Johnny Gruesome DEATH MASK!
The GRUESOME Mini-Movie starring Misty Mundae!
And the On-Line JOHNNY GRUESOME Comic Book!

Visit www.JohnnyGruesome.com

On the Brink of Extinction
by Shaun Jeffrey

Zach squeezed through the maw of the window, careful to avoid the teeth of glass jutting from the wooden gums.

He dropped to the floor and reached up to help Melinda as she followed him into the building.

"This had better be worth it," she said as she dusted herself off.

Ignoring the ire in her voice, Zach pulled a small torch (flashlight) out of his jeans pocket and switched it on. The narrow beam illuminated a small room with empty shelves and a door opposite. He walked across and eased it open to peer through the gap, heart hammering in case there was a security guard about.

Dim lights illuminated the enormous warehouse beyond, through which racks of shelves formed corridors. He breathed deeply, inhaling the aroma of dust and mildew, an aged smell that reminded him of abandoned buildings.

Although he couldn't spot anyone, Zach switched off his torch (flashlight)ch so as not to give away their presence, opened the door fully, and stepped into the room.

"Look at all this stuff," he said, keeping his voice low.

Melinda came and stood beside him. "As long as we can sell it, that's all that matters. I'm fed up of having no money."

"There's bound to be something. Look, it's massive. I bet we can find something of value to hock to Mickey at least."

"Well let's get a move on. I don't want to get caught."

Zach walked toward the nearest shelf when something caught his eye along the makeshift corridor. He turned to look, his jaw dropping.

Taking pride of place in the centre of the room stood a tyrannosaurus rex skull. A couple of other unrecognizable dinosaur skulls protruded from the wall like hunters trophies.

"Holy shit," Zach said.

"What is it?"

Zach pointed along the corridor. "Dinosaur bones."

"Great, I'll go fetch a dog, shall I. Bones are no bleedin' good."

Ignoring his girlfriend's comment, Zach approached the tyrannosaurus skull. He noticed wires attached to it and figured they were some sort of anti-burglar device like those attached to items in shops that set off an alarm if removed. Intrigued by the skull, he placed his right hand on the crazy crackled top, awed by the aged item beneath his fingers. The surface felt cool to the touch and the air around him shimmered as though looking through a hazy heat. Zach heard a faint humming sound that seemed to buzz inside his head. He felt dizzy. He snatched his hand back to steady himself and the feeling passed. His fingers tingled from the after-effects, and he flexed them a couple of times. What the hell---?

Cautious, he reached out, touching the dinosaur skull again. The air shimmered once more, and Zach felt dizzy , but this time he didn't yank his hand away. The colors of the room bled together, objects swimming in and out of focus, a multi-colored maelstrom. After a couple of seconds, the giddy sensation passed, and the blur of color started to coalesce.

Zach blinked staring wide-eyed, mouth open. He inhaled, choking on a fetid stench. All around him stretched primordial vegetation and trees. He looked up into a vivid blue sky streaked with meteorites that made a whooshing sound as they entered the atmosphere. A sharp cry drew his attention and a pterosaur flew over.

The sight was amazing.

In the distance, a herd of triceratops grazed the scrubland, making lowing sounds like cows, the calls echoing across the valley. Some of the group hung back, their movements uncoordinated. Blood gushed from injuries on the stragglers. Amid the herd, a couple of tyrannosaurus rex feasted, muscular jaws and jagged teeth tearing massive chunks from a carcass.

Right hand still on the tyrannosaurus skull, Zach looked back to now see the complete skeleton stretching into the grass, its rib cage a primitive pergola large enough to walk through.

A small bush waved in the breeze, its leaves tickling his ear. Zach ran his left fingers across the foliage, tearing off a leaf. What appeared to be blood speckled the rubbery surface. Zach grimaced.

A loud grumbling sound caught his attention and Zach looked up and stared at a vast orange ball of fire hurtling towards the Earth.

Terrified, Zach tore his hand from the skull, the scene melted away, and he found himself back in the warehouse.

He stepped away from the skull, legs shaking, ears ringing. Had he imagined it? Was the bone impregnated with a hallucinogenic substance? He raised his hand to wipe sweat from his face and saw the bloody leaf still grasped in his fingers.

The leaf looked and felt real; smelled real. But that was impossible.

"Jesus Christ. What the hell just happened?" Melinda asked.

Zach gulped to swallow the lump in his throat. "I … I …" He stared at the t-rex skull. Afraid the thing might open up and bite him, he took a step back.

Melinda looked scared. "You just disappeared. I swear to god, you vanished."

"I dunno. I touched that skull and it … I think I saw the moment when the meteorite wiped out the dinosaurs!"

Melinda looked at him as though he were crazy. "That's impossible."

"No shit." He held the piece of foliage out to her.

"Flowers would be nicer."

"No. Look at it. I just brought it back with me. I touched the skull and it, I don't know, transported me back in time."

She reached out, took the leaf out of his hand and stared at it. "Touch it. Touch the skull," he said.

Shrugging her shoulders, Melinda passed the piece of foliage back, stepped forwards and put her hand on top of the skull. "There. Now what?"

"Can you feel it?"

"Feel what? It's a skull." She removed her hand.

"Didn't anything happen? Didn't you feel giddy? Didn't you see anything?"

"I don't know what the hell happened before, but nothings happening. You touch it again."

Although wary, Zach stepped forwards and touched the skull, bracing himself for the dizzy sensation, but nothing occurred. "This is crazy. I touched that skull and I swear to God, the next thing I know, I'm back in the land of the bloody dinosaurs."

"Do you realise how stupid that sounds?"

"Well you explain it then. You said yourself I disappeared."

"I don't know what happened. Perhaps … perhaps I imagined it. I mean I wasn't really looking at you-" "Come here." He grabbed Melinda's arm and tugged her towards him. Then he placed his hand on top of the skull and waited. Melinda tried to pull free, but he gripped her tight.

Seconds ticked by.

Nothing.

Zach relaxed his hold and Melinda slipped out of his grasp.

He couldn't understand it. Why hadn't it happened again? He couldn't have imagined it, could he?

"Then where did the leaf come from?" he asked.

"How should I know? But I'll tell you what, I don't like this place, so the quicker we find some stuff to flog (steal and fence) the faster we can leave. Now come on."

Zach licked his lips and stared at the skull. He touched it, stroked it, patted it, but to no avail.

Confused, he stuffed the leaf in his pocket and followed Melinda into the next alcove.

Although Melindas had only just walked away, Zach couldn't spot her. Shelves of boxes blocked his sight. He approached the nearest carton and opened it to find an assortment of flints and primitive tools.

What the hell was this place? He'd assumed it was just a warehouse used to store electrical items, but this …

He put his hand in the box and pulled out a flint arrowhead, running his fingers across the serrated surface. Next to the box on the shelf, he spotted a stone axe and, like the tyrannosaurus skull, a couple of wires trailed from it. The wires snaked along the floor toward a shoebox-sized black box emitting a faint humming sound.

Zach warily reached out and touched the handle. As soon as his fingers made contact with the tool, the ringing started in his head, the air shimmered, the scene around him melted, and he found himself standing on a cliff. Snow blanketed the area and a cold wind blew. Zach wrapped his fingers around the axe to anchor himself and then turned to see a group of primitive men and women standing in the mouth of a cave, staring at him. They grunted something unintelligible, their prominent brows and heavyset features torn between puzzlement, fear and anger. Dressed in dirty furs, they pointed and chattered among themselves. One of them picked up a rock launching it overhand at Zach. The makeshift missile grazed his head, causing him to drop the axe. Again he rode the crazy merry-go-round of swirling color back to the storeroom. The stone axe lay at his feet.

Teeth chattering from the cold, he stooped, picked up the axe, needing to see whether it worked again. He curled his fingers around the shaft, but nothing happened.

He placed the axe back on the shelf and hurried ahead to find Melinda. Whatever this place was, they were out of here.

The next row contained artefacts of ethnic origin. Spears, bows, arrows and animal hide shields hung from the shelving, while alongside, display cases housed beads, drums, horns, pots and other paraphernalia. Wires snaked from a couple of the items.

Melinda stood bent over a display case, admiring tribal jewellery. She turned and looked up as Zach approached, her expression puzzled.

"Do you think this old tat is worth anything?" she asked.

Zach nodded. "Probably."

Before he could stop her, Melinda grabbed a necklace. Zach saw her blanch as though feeling sick; she vanished. One minute she was standing next to him, and the next she was gone..

About six seconds later, she reappeared, the necklace clattering as it landed on top of the display case. She stared at Zach, her mouth open, eyes wide in shock.

"I … I …" She shook her head.

"Now do you believe me?" Zach asked.

"What happened?"

"You disappeared. I don't know what it is or how it works."

"I was in a jungle village, surrounded by tribes' people who started shouting at me. That's when I dropped the necklace."

Zach nodded. "Yeah, losing contact with the item seems to bring you back."

Melinda reached out and gingerly touched the necklace again, but nothing happened.

"It only seems to work once for each item. See those wires? I think they're powering them, and when you touch something, it drains the power."

Melinda looked faint. Zach rushed back along the corridor and returned with a wooden seat that he'd noticed before. Melinda stared at it as though it might bite her.

"What if-"

"It hasn't got any wires attached to it so nothing's going to happen."

Shaking her head, Melinda collapsed onto the chair. "My god, it's unbelievable."

"That's one way of putting it."

"Do you know what this means? What we could do?"

Zach shrugged. "I haven't really thought about it."

"Everything in here's a gateway to the past. Jesus, we can travel through time. We can go … anywhere…steal anything." A sudden smile lit her face like a thousand watt bulb.

Zach didn't feel the same.

Melinda stood up, walked toward the next room. "Come on, I want to see where else there is."

"Forget it, we've got to get out of here," he said.

Melinda scowled at him. "No way."

Zach took a deep breath, trying hard to control the tsunami of panic sweeping over him. "Look, let's just go. I've got a bad feeling about this. We shouldn't be in here."

"Are you mad? I'm not going anywhere."

"I'm serious. We've got to go."

"So am I. This is our chance to be rich, and I'm not going to throw it all away because you've got a bad feeling."

Zach knew she was right, that he could be throwing away an untraceable fortune, but something ... something didn't sit well with him about all of this.

He turned, staring along another corridor, spotted a skeleton dressed in khaki trousers and jacket lying on the floor.

"Jesus," he said.

"What now?" Melinda groaned.

Zach pointed along the corridor.

"Is it real?" she asked.

Shrugging his shoulders, Zach walked towards it and crouched down to inspect the remains. Judging by its position, whoever it was had died where they fell. He ran a finger across the skull. What looked like dried blood splattered the front of the corpse's clothes.

Melinda screwed her face up. "How come no one's moved it?"

"Probably because no one knows it's here. Come on, we're going. Now."

"But how did he die?"

"I don't know and I don't care. We've got to go."

Despite her earlier protestations, Melinda followed without complaint and they exited the building the same way they'd entered.

Stars filled the black canvas sky above, and Zach took a deep breath. He felt glad to be out of the building.

" Shouldn't we tell someone? The body—" Melinda said.

Zach shook his head. "We do that and we admit we broke in. Someone'll find it one day."

As they walked across the bridge over the reservoir, Zach stuffed his hands in his pockets, felt the leaf he'd brought back from the past.

Not wanting any evidence of tonight, he dropped it into the water below. Fractal patterns of reflected silver from the overhead lights danced across the waters surface.

Next second, he started to cough and he covered his mouth with his hand. When the cough subsided, he removed his hand to see his palm speckled with blood.

The pain from a sudden headache hammered inside his skull.

At his side, Melinda started to cough too.

He recalled the herd of dinosaurs, remembered the blood soaked stragglers.

That's when everything fell into place.

The meteorite didn't kill the dinosaurs- they were already on the brink of extinction, wiped out by something else, something the eye couldn't see.

He stared at the water; saw the leaf sailing across the surface, propelled by the breeze like a small boat on its way to deliver a cargo that had taken millions of years to arrive.

∞∞∞

An Active member of the HWA, Jeffrey's 30-odd writing credits include short stories published in Surreal Magazine, Dark Discoveries, Shadowed Realms and DeathGrip: Legacy of Terror. Mr. Jeffrey also had one novel published entitled **'Evilution'**, *and a collection of short stories,* **'Voyeurs of Death'**. *He has another novel entitled,* **'Fangtooth'** *scheduled for publication late next year.*

Side Effects Will Occur
By Sheldon S. Higdon

At the back booth of the Revere Diner, Pete Warren leaned back and stretched his arm across his black Chesterfield overcoat draping his seat. His voice carried, drawing attention to himself as he spoke into his cell phone. A sign of self-importance.

"And make sure the paperwork is on my desk in the morning. Can you do that, Lauren? And if my wife calls tell her I'm in a meeting, and if Judge Thornberg calls, have him call my cell, I'd like to thank him for something." Pete glanced around at the customers, then at his Rolex. "Oh, and one last thing," he said, cupping his mouth and lowering his voice to a whisper. "Can you at least wear something more appropriate to work tomorrow? Y'know, something...I don't know...something that shows more curves Pant suits just don't do it for me."

Pete closed the cell phone, laying it next to an empty coffee cup and a plate of half-eaten cherry pie. He looked out the diner's window toward the Oasis Motel sitting across Route 6. White snowflakes obscured his view as though the truth were trying to hide behind the snowy façade. In fact, the Oasis Motel wasn't an oasis at all; it was a place where deals of a different kind took place and where business of a different sort happened. His look became a stare; his eyes remained focused, unblinking. A slight grin cut into his lower face, revealing white teeth, as carnal thoughts pounded his mind until a young waitress interrupted his private romp.

"Anything else, sir? A refill?" she said with a smile, holding a steaming coffee pot.

"How about your number?" Pete asked, looking her over.

"Excuse me?" her smile fading.

"Oh, nothing. Just thinking out loud," Pete said, his eyes assaulting her, peeling her uniform from her body. "Just a refill."

The waitress sloshed coffee into his cup, collected the remnants of his cherry pie, and tossed the check to the table as walking away without saying "thank you" or "come again."

An old woman, sitting across from a white-haired man in the next booth, peered over her companion's shoulder and glared at Pete. "Hmpf!" she snorted. She returned to her plate.

He ignored the woman, reached into the breast pocket of his Ralph Lauren shirt, and pulled out a little pink pill. He rolled it between his forefinger and thumb, admiring its candy-like appearance "Thanks, Judge Thornberg." He popped the little pink pill into his mouth, following it with a quick sip of coffee. He took another glance at his watch, withdrew a gold money clip from his pants pocket, and threw down a twenty. Rising from the booth, he grabbed his cell phone, put on his overcoat, and headed toward the parking lot, but skidded to a stop at the booth where the old woman sat sipping hot tea with the white-haired man.

"Y'know, sweetie, if you were thirty years younger...," Pete gave her a wink. "I'd be sitting in that seat instead of him." The old man looked at Pete for just a moment, smiled, and returned to his tea. As Pete strolled away, he heard the old woman scolding her partner. "So! This is how you stick up for me!" The white-haired man shook his head. "Nah, I've got plenty of tea!" he said.

Pete stepped into the falling snow, drawing his overcoat tightly around him. Although it was only mid-afternoon, the motel's neon sign flickered, barely legible through the snowfall, sparkling on and off. The 'O' and 'I' were burned out, the remaining letters spelling " as s Motel."

How appropriate, Pete thought. His Cadillac sat at the far end of the motel's gravel lot, snow blanketing the expensive car, as thought his car, too, was incognito. Not that Joy, his wife, would be out this far from Pittsburgh and see it, but nonetheless, Pete wouldn't be out this far either if he thought she had the slightest chance of catching him.

Pete had married his high school sweetheart twenty-five years ago. Joy had been there from day one, when he was a struggling lawyer trying to prove himself, to when he won the election to Superior Court Judge. Together they'd lived a good life; a house in Pittsburgh, another in South Carolina. Together they'd raised three children, spoiled one grandchild, and babied two dogs. But Pete had a big appetite, and with big bucks, comes big pleasures. Pete stuck his hands deep into his wool overcoat and headed toward the Oasis.

* * *

She spat her gum into the small wastebasket by the dresser, which doubled as the television stand in the drab motel room. Giving herself the once over in the wall mirror by the bathroom, she primped her blonde hair, dabbing her makeup with tissue. "Lookin' good, girl," she said, tossing the tissue into the wastebasket.

She made her way to the king-sized bed, slid her fur coat over, sat on the mattress' edge, and began bouncing. Her breasts rose and fell, keeping rhythm as she went up and down a few times.

"Good. Not a squea-"

A knock from the motel door halted her bed test.

"Don't be nervous now," she whispered to herself, straightening her tight white skirt. "He's a regular."

She opened the door. Pete stood in the cold air, his shoulders hunched to his ears.

"Well hello, Judge. Thought maybe you wasn't coming, but you will be soon, if you know what I mean?" She giggled.

"Jesus. How many times have I told you not to call me 'Judge'?"

She rolled her eyes. "Whatever, it's your dime."

Pete entered the room and closed the door behind him, shaking off the chill.

Grabbed him by the shoulders, she pressed herself against him, licked her lips and locked her blue eyes onto his. "Are you gonna throw the book at me? I've been naughty, y'know."

Pete smiled. "Depends on the charges."

She leaned in, ran her pink tongue across his lips, pushing him back until he dropped on the bed.

"Let's see what I can come up with."

She grabbed the remote from the nightstand, "Maybe lewd conduct." She flicked on the television. "So you relax and get warmed up while I get into something more...deviant." She handed Pete the remote and disappeared into the bathroom. Pete scooted back, leaning against the cheap headboard.

On the television screen, a smiling man in a suit was speaking.

"Looking to rekindle your marriage? Then Erectasin is the choice for you. It's guaranteed or your money back. Just remember, the pink pill is a phone call away. And for only thirty-nine ninety-five you can't afford not to call. Five, five, five, Pink Pill. Call now! If not for you, then for her. Side effects will occur if--"

"It's definitely not for her," Pete said to himself, changing the

Shroud Classifieds:

"Looking for high grade opium and a dark-spirited nineteen-year-old to share it with me..."

ask for "Hiram"

www.hiramgrange.com

channel. He could feel the ever-present need growing, the want for climax, the addictive weight between his legs that he knew all men feel. However, the increased pressure felt more stark, more intense, a scraping want for release. Was it the little pink pill? "Just a forewarning," he yelled. "I've taken a little pink buddy to give me some extra boost."

The bathroom door opened a crack, "Is that a promise?"

"All I can say is, that if you're not bow-legged now, cowgirl, you will be." The thought of impending orgasm increased the weight in his scrotum, the growing need to seed.

"Yee-haw!" she said, closing the door.

Pete flipped through the channels, stopping on a live local news report from the Court Building in downtown Pittsburgh. His mouth's playful smile faded into a surprised gaping hole of amazement as he watched the event unfold on the screen.

A female reporter stood inside an ornate marbled hallway, people in suits passing behind her. Lights shone brightly on her as she spoke.

"It seems that Judge Aaron Thornberg, while on his lunch break, was caught soliciting sex from an undercover Pittsburgh police officer on the corner of Reno Avenue. This was a sting operation by the police department to catch "Johns" and prostitutes in action, to curtail an ongoing problem. As you know, the Mayor has demanded the police reduce crime within our city, and it appears the police force is doing its job well. The chief has stated that the department will work unceasingly until prostitutes and their customers are eradicated from the city, regardless of position..."

The bathroom door opened, and she walked in, wearing only red silk stockings, garters, and matching high heels. She had redone her makeup. Her skin was light brown like creamed coffee, caramel smooth. Her blonde hair hung loosely to her shoulders, swaying in rhythm with her round, firm breasts. She drifted in front of the television, feeling like a Roman Goddess, statuesque and beautiful.

"Will this get me twenty-five-to-life, Judge?" she asked.

Sweat trickled down Pete's pale face. His eyes were wide, fixed on the TV. Not once did he look at her. The opportunity for sex and immediate gratification continued, but retreated into a dark recess, trampled by another realization.

She bent over, jiggling her breasts to get his attention. "Looky, they're fleeing the scene of a crime." She arched back up, trying to draw his attention toward her flexibility.

"Move," he said, waving his hand at her. "I can't see the TV!"

"What the fuck's wrong with you?" she asked. "That lump pointing at me from your pants and your lack of attention is giving me mixed damn signals."

He leaned around her to get a better view of the newscast, but she countered by pressing the power button. The image vanished. "Why'd you do that?" Pete jumped up from the bed and pulled out his money clip. "I can't do this. I gotta go!" He stuffed in his shirt tail, attempted to adjust his swelling member.

"What!" she said. "Go where? Jesus Christ, Pete! Wha--."

Pete tossed the entire money clip to her. "Keep it," he said and opened the motel door, allowing a shot of cold air and snow to intrude.

"You can't just go!" she said. "What's happened? Is it something I did--?"

"No! I just can't get caught doing this. I simply can't. It'll look like--" Pete stepped into the stiffening chill, closing the door behind him. He hoped the cold would douse the heated swell between his legs.

She stood in the room alone, hair blown a mess, nipples erect, confusion and anger melding across her face. She counted the money, folded it, returned it to the clip. Her lips parted, sneering. She yanked the sheet off the bed, wrapped it around herself, and opened the door, stomping out onto the second level of the motel. She ran to the end where Pete was brushing snow off his Cadillac, leaned over the railing.

"Judge! What the hell?"

He ignored her, continued scraping the ice and snow from the Cadillac's windshield.

"You're gonna regret this, Judge! You'll be back! They always come back." She held up the gold money clip. "Besides, Judge Pete Warren, you've got an addiction and I'm the dealer! And I've got your money clip!"

A ringing came from within Pete's pant pocket. He pulled out his cell phone, flipped it open, checking the caller ID. "Shit!" he said, repocketed it, unanswered. He threw the snow scraper into the back seat of his car. "Pawn it," he yelled up at her. "You should be able to get something for it." He pulled out his keys and opened the driver's side door.

Her face changed from its cocky glow to a stone cold glare. She pulled the money from the clip. "I don't need your fucking handouts!" She threw the clip at the car; it hit the back window and bounced into the snow. "I earn my money, Judge!"

Pete ignored her remarks and got inside the car, easing himself into the driver's seat, aware of the raging stiffness in his pants. He turned the key, the engine came to life, spitting white smoky plumes into the cold air. The Cadillac backed up, slowly, and then pulled forward only to stop when he came to the edge of the lot where it met Route 6.

"Judge!" she screamed, opening the sheet and exposing herself. "You'll be back!" She shook her breasts back and forth. "They always come back!"

The Cadillac pulled out, fading into the distance, leaving her standing, alone and forgotten.

* * *

Pete had driven twenty minutes when his cell phone rang again. Like the previous few times it had chimed, he ignored it. He would tell his wife that the meeting ran longer than expected, and that Lauren didn't relay any of his messages to him or he would have gotten back to her.

The car's wipers swatted at the snow that continued to fall. The rigidity in his trousers remained, a tentpole of manliness that, had he not been so frightened, would have made him very proud. He had to get rid of it; the intense need for climax was still present, painful.

Pete allowed his brain to numb for a moment, thinking of baseball, adding rows of numbers. He rocked back and forth like a schooner caught in a New England Nor'easter. He thought of the old woman in the diner.

Sudden nausea hit Pete as heat seared the length of his penis and shot into his testicles. He shifted in his seat, trying to relocate his taut manhood into a more comfortable position, trying to ease the agony. And for a moment, he thought he smelled something... had he ejaculated? No, it was... burning. Pain struck him. He grimaced. His penis felt as if it were being used as some sort of fleshy flamethrower; he unbuttoned his pants, unzipping his fly to allow the feeling of lava pouring through it escape. Sweat beaded on his forehead. He pushed a button, lowering the window, letting cold air and snow into the car. The air felt good.

"What the hell's happening?" Pete asked no one, pushing on his crotch.

He looked in the rearview mirror, giving himself the once over. His face appeared pale, revealing a milky tinge beneath his normal tanned appearance. He stuck out his tongue. Nothing unusual. He widened both of his eyes, pulling his lower lids down, one at a time; nothing.

What the fuck's happening?

He wiped his face with the back of his arm and then began rubbing his sore penis. The painful burning was becoming continuous, spiny, prickles, like jolts of electricity. Edison or Tesla would have never dreamed of anything like it.

"Son of aaaah bitch! Is it a goddamn kidney stone? Fuck!"

Pete rubbed with fervor, trying to relieve the pain, the electric bolts continuing, becoming sharper, unbearable.

The snow was falling heavier and harder. Pete struggled to keep the car on the road.

Through squinting eyes, he spied a sign announcing an emergency pull off area a mile down the road. He pressed hard on the gas pedal, the car's tires laboring in the slush for purchase.

He continued rubbing his crotch. "Oh God, please, hurry! I'm coming fire!"

He sped down the highway, passing other cars, when the pain suddenly stopped. Pete released a long, shuddering moan of relief. Jesus, he thought. Thank you Jesus. His scrotum felt strange, as thought he'd been robbed of a long-teased and promised orgasm. Oh, God, what a mess I've made. What a mess I've made of everything.

A wave of unexpected nausea blanketed him.

Something warm oozed down his inner thighs. His lower extremities felt as though they were melting, like hot candle wax. He put his hand down and felt around his crotch. He touched something wet. His stomach lurched again, and his breathing became shallow. He pulled out his hand; it was covered in crimson goo.

The emergency pull off was in sight, behind it a billboard stood, advertising a product Pete's frantic mind couldn't quite make out, but seemed familiar with.

He stood on the Cadillac's brakes, skidding through the gravel emergency area, coming to a stop before the billboard. He slammed the shift into park, hopped out, leaving the Cadillac idling and quickly pulled down his pants and boxers. Horns blared as more cars crawled by, his display something to ogle other than the dull, snow-encrusted road. He ignored them, bending over, peering at his manhood.

Pete's crotch boiled in thick blood, smearing his inner thighs, matting his body hair. His body shook with revulsion and icy dread. His eyes filled with tears. He began clearing away the hot, red viscosity with trembling hands. Weak, he fell against the car, sliding until his bare ass met cold snow. Tears streamed down his face. He felt around, trying to find his pride and joy, but found nothing.

Pete cried, bare-assed in the cold snow along Route 6. The snow fell. Questions bounced in his head as cars passed by. No one stopped. How would he explain this to Joy? Am I going to die? Pete wasn't sure he wanted to live. His penis melted! Yet, lurking in his scrotum, in the center of his being, the need for release, the want of orgasm remained, buzzing in his body, tapping at his mind.

Somewhere his wife, Joy, sat waiting for him. Somewhere, at the Oasis Motel, SHE waited for him to come back because they always came back.

"My God," Pete screamed. "I'm a fucking Ken doll!"

The billboard, ignored, looming above Pete's head, displayed an ad for *Erectasin*, proclaiming its power, as well as to heed its warning that—

"side effects will occur."

∞∞∞∞∞

Sheldon S. Higdon *has had work appear in numerous publications ranging from fiction to non-fiction. His short stories have recently been published in Shroud Magazine and future works will be appearing in Werewolf Magazine, and the upcoming Anthology of the Living Dead. He's also had feature articles appear in the Summerguide 2008 issue of the Portland Magazine as well as their forthcoming September, 2008 issue. See what Sheldon S. Higdon is up to at www.myspace.com/sheldonhigdon.*

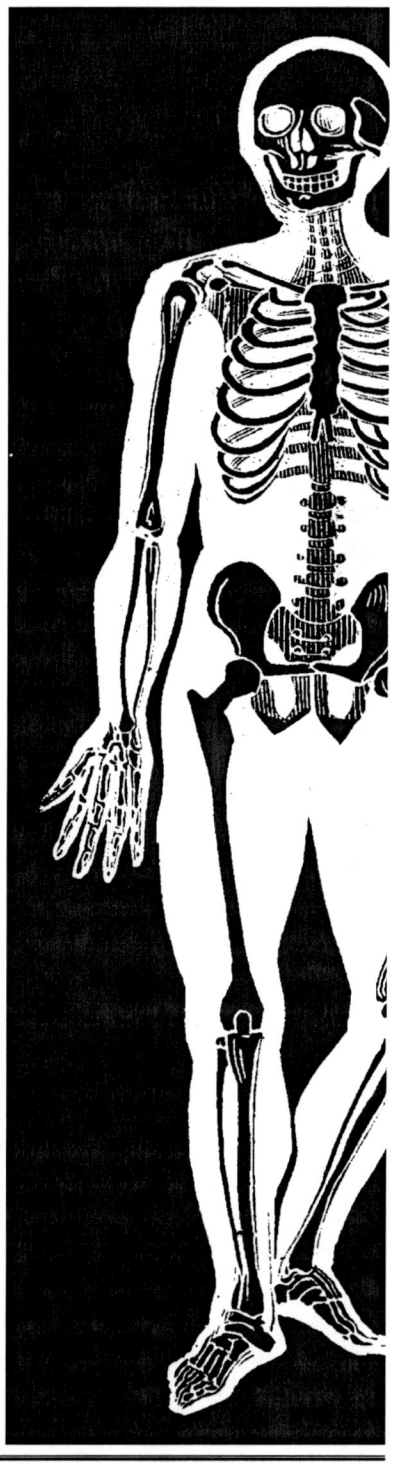

NOBLE SINCERE

by jeff jewett

"Music is the taking of a soul when the body don't want to give it up, you see. That's why music moves you. And lookie here, Lawd help the man who won't be moved, Danny. It don't mean he ain't got no soul, no sir, ev'rybody got a soul, see. It only means when that soul get up to go, the body won't have the know-how nor the strength to stop it."

Danny sat on the edge of a milk crate, his posture erect, an Albert System clarinet poised at his lips. As only an eleven-year-old can, his wide eyes watered with awe as he looked up at Noble Sincere sitting on the giant bed.

The taking of a soul when the body don't want to give it up...

Danny dipped this new piece of knowledge into his imagination as though it were a piece of cornbread dipped into a bowl of jambalaya.

He stirred the thought.

* * *

The sign for the Wrought Iron Fence Motel was barely visible beyond shrub and vines. So was the iron fence out front. The property had not a scrap of wrought iron. It was cast iron. Wrought iron was expensive, and the establishment rented exclusively to Negroes.

He had been walking home from school when he heard someone playing the clarinet. He carried his own clarinet, so proud of it that he wouldn't conceal the instrument in a case even if he'd had one. The melody lured him to a two-story motel, its' stucco cracked and chipped. At first, Danny had thought the place haunted. His head slightly tilted as he regarded the balcony, which had a subtle slump, and too many shutters from the windows were missing; as a result, the face of the motel appeared uneven and somehow lopsided. As he regarded a single dehydrated cypress tree, he shivered. It appeared too long for the swamp as its branches lurked above the motel and swept the roof.

He'd stood in front of the cast iron gate and listened, while somewhere beyond one of the windows on the first floor, a master musician played a clarinet. After a long moment, a stand-up bass, the rhythm catchy and lethargic, produced clean thumps from a second floor window. Below, on the first floor, a stick-less toilet plunger muted the bell of a trumpet producing a nagging whine as though in complaint about being awoke. Then, a bullying baritone Sax warned them they had all better shut up. Danny laughed heartily as a melodic debate began and blended into a collaborative musical conversation. It's wonderful, he thought. It was the sound of New Orleans. Abruptly the music stopped.

"Who goes there, I say out front?"

"Who me? I'm Danny, sir. I go to Lincoln."

A dark shadow stepped from the motel onto the walkway. A man black as the shadow from which he emerged stood in front of the doorway. Bald, he wore a tank top t-shirt, suspenders hanging around his trousers. Feebly, the old man drew near the gate.

"Is that an Albert I see?"

"Yessir." Danny displayed

the clarinet like an offering. "Last month my ma-ma sent it to me all the way from New York. She's house cleaning there for some rich folks. "

"I see. Can you play?"

"Yessir. I've been sort of finding my way. Even though I ain't had no lessons."

"Lessons? Boy, do you even know what music is?"

Danny had no reply.

"Well son, answer me this. Can you ketch?" And the old man had smiled a toothless smile.

* * *

Noble Sincere had been born a slave. He occupied room #5 on the first floor at The Wrought. As a young man, he had run free and traveled the world as a Clarinetist playing blues and ragtime. In all his years, Noble Sincere had never taught music, for he believed playing music was like freedom; you have to first find it and then take it.

Danny sat on a crate in room number five. Like a hooked fish, the boy had caught a taste of know-how and squirmed in his seat hungry for more. "So if I wanted to, I could blow this here clarinet, and pull a man's soul right out from his body?"

"Pull it out," Noble Sincere squeaked with amusement. "Then wha' would you do with it, chile'?"

"Don' know. Put it in a jar, I guess"

"Like your ma-ma's preserves, I reckon."

"Naw," Danny said, "I'd break the jar. So it'd be free."

Noble Sincere froze, his eyes narrowed as a man watching a bobber making ripples in a still pond. He let out a loud, choppy, crackling laugh, like the sound of trampled on pecan shells. On the thick mattress, he rocked back and forth until finally tiring, and then leaning forward with his elbows on his knees, he lowered his head and sighed.

"Put it in a jar. Boy, you are beyond one."

Noble Sincere sat up, wiped his eyes, and silently regarded Danny for a moment.

"Now son, let's see what you got. Let me hear sum' those scales."

Danny straightened his back; his fingers stumbled onto their correct position; left thumb on ring pointed at two o'clock; right first finger over the bottom trill key; both little fingers on long keys. Finally, Danny gently bit down atop the mouthpiece and blew notes that were diluted with the passage of too much air.

Noble Sincere's face scrunched up on one side as the other side squinted. This boy's finger technique is troublesome, Noble thought. And listen to that air. As Noble's face thawed, he mumbled, "But I reckon this here chile' will surely do."

* * *

But for the sloppy sound of musical scales that rose up and down, the apartment in which Danny lived was quiet. His Aunt worked at a local restaurant and she was hardly ever home. Danny had funneled his loneliness and longing for his mother into

dedicating himself in learning to play the clarinet. Practicing in his Aunt's small house, the character of sound was lonely. The next day, however, he was excited since after returning home from school and finishing chores, he would go back to the motel.

From back of a streetcar, he again realized just how good he was getting at playing the clarinet. "If he liked my scales," he mumbled, "wait till he gets a load of my Twinkle-Twinkle Little Star."

Before the streetcar came to a complete halt, he jumped off and ran the distance to The Wrought Iron Motel.

* * *

Last weeks musical conversation that had been jolly had changed into talk of a serious matter. It was as if a calling connected Danny to his origin, digging into his inner being, as though he were standing in front of a West African village where he listened to the sound of pulsating drums. From beyond the window of the hotel, he heard the overlapping, popping, and slapping of various drums as they blended into a single fabric of sound. Driving and dreadful, the tempo was hasty and reckless, growing faster and faster. Although the strong energy called out to him, Danny was afraid to answer.

'Lawd help the man who won't be moved, Danny.'

He opened the cast iron gate, stepped onto the walkway, and hesitantly entered The Wrought Iron Motel.

Inside, the sound was deafening. Though Danny wanted to flee, he bravely hugged his clarinet, frantically running down the hallway that seemed much too long for the interior of such a small hotel. In contrast to the thumping sounds that surrounded him, the boy timidly knocked on room number five.

An old woman who was as black as an abyss answered the door. As if to enhance her blackness, she wore a white robe and head kerchief. Her eyes blazed down at Danny. Then the effort of a smile betrayed her eyes. Danny and the women regarded one another. The smile, Danny realized, was not sincere. As though she too had summed up the boy, she retreated into the candle lit room, leaving the door ajar.

A red blanket hung over the window that prevented sunlight from pouring in; as a result, a pinkish ray of light framed a slanted rectangle on the wood floor. A giant bed had been pulled away from the wall. Burning candles surrounded it. Within the circle, a variety of elaborate designs decorated the floor. The designs, he noticed, were ugly. Danny stood next to the window inside the pink light, and distanced himself from the elaborate designs, the old women, and death.

Noble Sincere lay on the giant bed with his arms atop a white sheet, which slowly rose up and down with each struggling breath. Beneath his arms, resting across his chest, he held an ancient clarinet. His rheumy eyes looked at Danny.

The old woman in white stood at the foot of the bed. She held what appeared to be a twig. As in the letter Y, she raised her arms and chanted something Danny could not hear; and snapped the twig in two. Instantly, the beating of the drums simmered into a low rumble like the sound of falling rain.

The old women in white ordered, "Boy Dan-nee, you go blow ta' candles from the dressar."

Danny inched out of the pinkish light and into the shallow dark. On top the dresser, he saw a variety of small bottles, various fruit, and statues of Saints. Eleven candles burned. He took a breath to blow the candles out; however, as a mere puff of breath escaped his lungs; the candles extinguished. A residue of smoke burst from the candles like water from a busted levee, and the small room filled with a white, mellow haze. Like a ballet performed on a stage of pinkish light, Danny watched the swirling wisps of smoke dance and weave. His legs began to feel light, and he smiled as he listened to the rumble of drums. Danny heard a rattle and his smile faded. It was the old woman in white, shaking a rattle above Noble Sincere's feet. Danny heard a voice within the rhythm of drums.

"Step on in the circle, Danny. Let me git a look at ya, son."

Danny turned his gaze away from the old woman and onto Noble Sincere as the old man beckoned the boy to move closer.

"Tick-tock, son."

Cautiously, Danny stepped inside the circle. With that first step, the old woman in white began to chant. He looked down into the eyes of Noble Sincere.

"I've been sick an awful long time."

Danny had no reply.

"This here place, The Wrought, that's what colored folks call it. You know why, son?"

Danny listened to the drums; he heard patterns in the rhythm, as though they contained meaning.

"See, wrought is what you do, son. A man's livelihood, his trade, you see. That's the meanin' of the word."

Danny listened for meaning in the patterns of rhythm.

"See, playin' music is the tellin' of a tale, son. A tellin' of sorrow, of joy, of life, Danny. That's what musical instumints' foe. Tellin' the tales of life. That's my trade. My undertakin', see. That's my wrought."

As though the woman's limbs were struggling for supremacy of her body and rebelling against her brain, the old woman in white began to dance an ancient dance, elbows and knees thrusting inward and then outward, head bowed, then raised, eyes closed as though in ecstasy. Danny ignored her.

His attention was on Noble and the juggling rhythms of the drums. As if a language, he could almost make out words within the rhythms, true words, real words. Slower, Danny thought. Why can't they play slower, so I can understand what they're sayin'? Play slower so I can understand your words.

"Danny? What is music?"

The boy glanced at the old woman in white. Then he stared down into the eyes of Noble Sincere.

"The taking of a soul when the body don't wanna give it up."

Noble Sincere bit down on his clarinet and played. Danny's shoulders slumped. His heart swelled. His brow furrowed, tears squeezing from his eyes. He heard. He listened. Finally.

He understood.

In the melody, the beautiful melody, every note was a word. True words. Real words. Words he understood. He heard a tale about boy who, from bondage into freedom, had loved and been loved. He heard a tale about anger and injustice; a tale about a free man who celebrated the newfound freedom of other men; and an adventure about a young man, who for the first time had tasted equality while playing the Blues in France. Danny heard every word to the end, when finally, a non-existent note, perhaps not from the clarinet but from somewhere ancient and dark, slurred his name. "Daaannnneeee."

Noble Sincere's body sagged, the clarinet falling onto his chest, the sheet deflating into his last exhalation.

The rumble of drums intensified to the sound of thunder.

The old woman handed Danny an unlidded Mason jar. "'Ere it come boy. Prepare."

White and watery substance appeared from the bell of the ancient clarinet. As he had watched the wispish smoke swirl in the ray of pinkish light, so too did Danny stare as the white and watery seeped out and away from the ancient clarinet.

"It's his offerin' chile'. Take de jar and catch it. Catch-it. Take it!"

The tempo of the drums grew faster and louder.

In the smoke-filled room, the white and watery hovered above the bed like a soggy sheet of paper floating in a slow current of polluted water. The size of a handkerchief, its boundless shape changed and turned inside itself, shimmering and twisting, like a sea creature making its way to the surface. Dreamily, it continued to float up and away.

"Take dis' jar boy! Don't let 'tit git ta'way. You must catch it and take it. Act!"

From the ceiling protruded a single light bulb; a short thin chain made of tiny beads hung from its base. As if in a hypnotic trance, Danny watched the billowing white and watery rise up and up as it slowly floated toward the short chain that hung from the light fixture.

The beating of the drums cracked like lighting, the tempo was a blur.

"EYEEEEEE! Foolish chile! Tit dis' gone!"

Danny, careful not to drop his own clarinet, grabbed the

Mason jar with his free hand and jumped atop the bed. He leapt and swept the jar over his head just missing the bulb, the small thin chain swung back and forth.

"Dis lid boy. Take dis lid."

He caught the lid with his clarinet hand and slapped it onto the jar.

"Eye! You got 'tit boy! Indeed, you got 'tit!"

As though the world had instantly become deaf, the drums stopped. Danny stood atop the bed, looked into and through the jar. He saw nothing except the old woman's reflection on the other side; her intense, calculating eyes contorted and twisted. Broadening across her face was a hideous, warped grin. This time, Danny realized, the smile was sincere.

"You can give ' tit ta' me boy." She said sweetly, "Ida can keep tit safe for you. Though you must offer tit freely."

Danny held the jar up and away from the old woman, defending it.

"I shall have't for me collection, yes? Offer it to me."

She shrieked, her arms pleading out to Danny. Off the bed and into the long hall, he ran outside. He made a sharp detour from the walkway that led him toward the back of the motel. He ran where the old cypress longed to be, on a path that led to the swamp.

* * *

In the dry shade on the grassy edge of the swamp, the boy leaned against a cypress and mourned. He mourned Noble Sincere. He mourned for his mother in New York who he dearly missed. He mourned for himself because he had been so afraid. He mourned as though he could still hear the melody, that beautiful melody and the words. He looked through and into the jar and saw nothing except his palm. He wondered why that old witch had wanted it so badly if nothing was inside? Speaking to the jar, Danny said," You sure can play, Mr. Sincere."

He lifted the jar over his head, throwing it against the cypress. The jar shattered with the lid still intact with jagged edges of glass. For a long moment, nothing happened.

Danny licked his lips, raised his clarinet to his mouth. He could not taste the clarinet for it was part of him now. Smooth as a gunslinger's draw, his fingers took their rightful position. He did not close his eyes, yet his eyes saw nothing. His lungs were virgin to the graceful way they expanded and deflated, the grace of an ocean tide sliding in and then retreating from the shore. Danny Mills stood at the grassy edge of the mucky swamp, played a melody beyond all limits of what else in the world; each note a word; the captivating beginning of a life long tale.

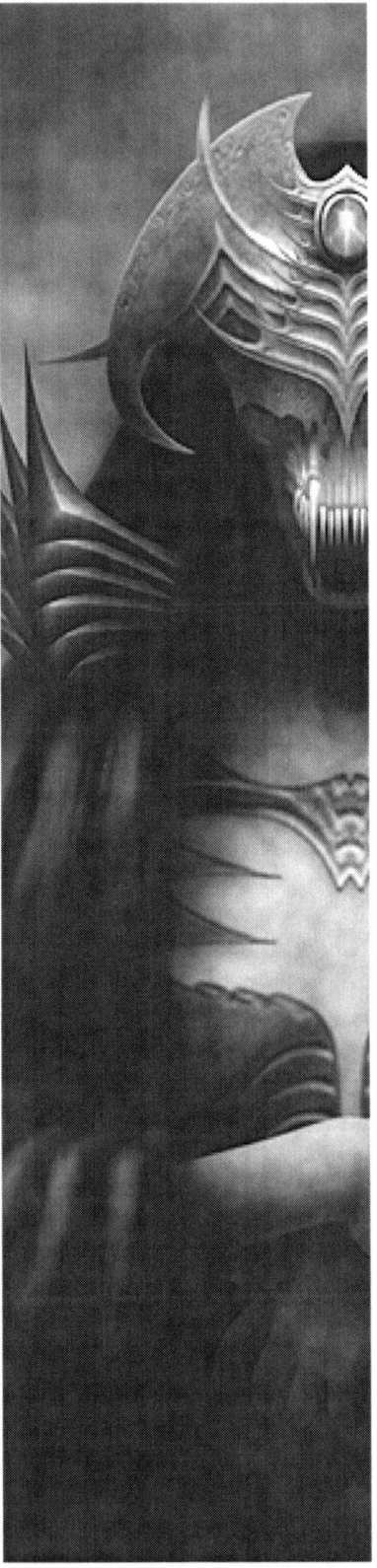

BLUE MOON FEVER
BY TINA L. JENS

It was Friday the 13th, and we were all suffering from Blue Moon Fever, to boot.

You know what a Blue Moon is, don't you? I don't mean when a second full moon shines in a month, real Blue Moon standards, that's commonplace stuff. I mean that ever-so-rare event when the moon actually glows blue – happens 'bout twice a decade. Scientists will tell you that dust in the atmosphere at very high altitudes causes it, or the selective absorption of moonlight by soot particles of the right size. But that's all scientist talk.

You don't have to understand it, 'cause logic goes right out the window when a Blue Moon shines in. It throws that filmy Blue-cheese haze over everything, and causes reality to shift off kilter. You layer that smelly bit of astronomy onto the black astrologic implications of a Friday the 13th – then the creepy crawlies come climbing out of whatever hellhole or alternate reality they've been hiding in. Nothin' you can do about it. Might as well sign up for the Universal Studios' Creature Feature Monster Mash Movie Marathon tour.

The whole country had been infested with monsters, maybe the whole world. Oddly enough, the supernatural infestations had segregated regionally, and they were pretty strict about not crossing each other's boundaries.

The Rockies and other mountainous regions had been hit with a plague of ghosts; except for the Appalachians and the Ozarks. They had h'aints. (I wasn't too clear on what the difference was.) They weren't just haunting houses. News reports were documenting spirit-infested schools, poltergeist-plagued pools, haunt-filled horticultural centers, and a corporeally challenged charge on the local K-Mart.

For some reason, the witches had all congregated in Wichita, before hitting the rails to torment the major train towns.

The vampires vamoosed to the southwest. I figured that was because vamps were a lot like snakes – bad blood circulation – so they liked to stay where it was warm.

The New England states had been mobbed by mummies. I guess that salt sea air shored up the embalming and preservatives and stuff.

The zombies were stumbling up and down the West coast,

concentrating in San Fran, L.A. and Hollyweird. I never did figure that one out, 'cause I'd read somewhere that a zombie would return to his grave if you fed him salt, so I didn't understand how they could be taking over the surfing circuit. But maybe it's the iodine in iodized table salt that makes zombies so loopy. In that case, a little salt water wouldn't hurt them, and might even wash away some of those pesky critters that tend to take up habitation in a corpse.

The Midwest? We got the werewolves. I'd have chalked that choice up to the wide open spaces and rolling plains – plenty of room for the big dogs to run – except the majority of them were chasing cars on the Magnificent Mile in the Windy City. Go figure!

So on the most dangerous night of the millennium (Blue Moon Fever and Friday the 13th don't often align – thank whatever gods you honor), was I triple-locked into my fourth floor apartment in a building with a secure lobby and no trees within jumping distance from my window, safe and sound from the werewolf threat?

Of course not. I was at McGees, my regular Friday night hangout, watching the Mini-Reubens (a damn good snack and a pretty good band).

Now it'd be a pretty logical question to ask why such a meatable, carnivore-inviting named group was out tempting fate on a night like this? Blame it on the tequila. Blame it on the doobie. Blame it on the rock -n- roll. But no hairy-palmed, flea-bitten, rabid dog-boy was going to get in the way of our happening, baby.

"El Nino" was blowin' electric guitar solos across the stage like gusts from a hurricane. Rockin' Rob was layin' down that marbles-in-the-mouth, "Feelin' Alright" Joe Cocker groove. "King Velvet," a Presley-impersonator ('cept he played electric bass) was dropping bass bombs and Elvis-pelvis moves in the unlikeliest of places. And "Falsetto Pheel," who doubled as back-up singer and percussionist, was channeling 1960's Charlie Watts – but on a night like this, what else would you expect?

The band kicked things off with CCR's "Bad Moon Rising," Presley's "Blue Moon of Kentucky," and the Marcel's "Blue Moon," (you know, the one that goes "dang-a-dang-dang, ding-a-dong-ding") and that was just to open the show! They were promising the entire soundtrack to An American Werewolf in London for the second set.

I didn't know if they were tempting fate or pacifying the spirits, but there were no jugular-spray, throats-ripped-out, werewolf-massacres during the first two hours.

During the break, as a kind of public service announcement, Shanli, the waitress, climbed up on a chair and reviewed the ways to kill a werewolf.

Somebody suggested we toss them what was left of the garlic chicken blue plate special, since nobody had ordered it, anyway. The manager wasn't too pleased about the suggestion, so he was pretty quick to point out that garlic only worked on vampires.

Scott, one of the regulars, yelled out, "Werewolves are just big dogs, right? Mebbe they'll choke on the chicken bones!"

That got a big laugh from everybody but the manager and Shanli. She was tryin' to hide it, but she was scared. Maybe the rest of us should have been too, but the bar had been serving all drinks half-price, so we'd pretty well pickled our nerves and our brains.

Finally, Shanli climbed down and quit trying. She just shook her head, mumbled something about us all deserving to get turned into dog-meat, and went and turned the juke box up.

The only serious werewolf deterrent anybody in the bar could come up with was silver bullets. Now, I won't pretend there weren't any guns in the room – this was Chicago after all – but the gun-toters didn't have any silver bullets. Cop Killers and synthetics, yes. Silver – no.

We had one silver-plated switchblade and three-and-a-half pairs of sterling silver earrings (Big Love, the front waiter, chipped in the half). But the microwave wasn't going to melt the metal, and it's not like we had a bullet mold, even if it did...

* * *

So we were shit out of luck when the mangy pack of werewolves broke through the plate glass window at two A.M. They were wearing matching, severely-distressed, black leather jackets. The backs of the jackets were all painted with the words "Moon Mad Mongrels" in kind of a half-circle over the picture of a werewolf sitting on his haunches, howling at a full moon. They sported all the bad habits that you'd expect when you combined a motorcycle gang and a wolf pack; including a fondness for matching red T-shirts so ripped and faded you could just barely read the slogan, "Born to be Bad."

We took one look at the silver chains (heavy enough to tow a truck) hanging from their shoulder lapels like silk scarves on a designer trench coat, and gave up on the whole silver-as-a-weapon idea.

The wolves had their mouths all set for a blood frenzy cocktail; shaken, not stirred.

The leader of the pack – his jacket said "Rare Were" – grabbed Big Love and placed his drink order, "A Mary – heavy on the blood, easy on the Tabasco and bile," he growled. You could still see the wolf's claw-marks on Big Love's arms as he hurried to fill the order.

A big silver-haired fellow with clipped ears and a gold hooped earring shoved a guy out of a seat and across the room, so he could sit down beside me.

"I'm Loupe de do Garou, who are you?" he crooned.

"I'm sure as hell not little Red Riding Hood," I told him.

"And I'm not Big Bad," he snickered. He pointed his paw at a wolf in purple leathers across the room. "He's over there. But I do like little girls, especially blond ones," he said, sniffing at my locks like we were part of a bad seventies shampoo commercial.

I figured he was gonna eat me right then and there, until he started waxin' rhap-so-dic about the June moons and spooning tunes. So his line was corny and his vocabulary old-fashioned (Obviously he'd been out of circulation for awhile). But every girl likes a little romance, and my first lost love had been a long-haired biker boy and in bar light, boy and wolf can look pretty much the same. I was just about to write my number on a bar napkin for him when one of his buddies barged in, breaking the mood.

This beast had breath fouler than creamed carrion. I nearly fell off my chair from the odor when he leaned over me, saying, "Hey Garou, trouble's brewing at the bar. You ready to rumble and tumble?"

Loupe de do Garou bared his fangs and growled, "I'm busy here."

The new dog barked, "Who's the chick?" Then he poked at me, putting his paws where they didn't belong and said, "Tender little morsel, isn't she?"

Loupe snarled at the familiarity. He looked like he was about to take a swipe out of his buddy.

I spoke up to stop the trouble before it started, "Jeannie," I said.

"Like comes in a bottle!" the interloper wisecracked, then laughed at his own joke.

Loupe said to me, "This mangy cur is Wolfman-You-Can-Call-Me-Jack. He's completely hyphenated – both in brain and name."

To Wolfman-You-Can-Call-Me-Jack he said, "Scram. Go play with Moonstruck and Shaggy. I'm busy."

WYCCM-Jack whined and slinked off with his tail between his legs.

I'd spotted Moonstruck – he had a silver shock of hair that ran right down the middle of his scalp. He'd super-glued it into spikes. I couldn't spot Shaggy, but Loupe pointed him out at the bar. His hair was perfect.

Tensions were building in the room – you could hear curses and growls exchanged, all a big display of testosterone and posturing between wolves and men. But I didn't worry about it. I wasn't the bouncer, and Loupe de do Garou was nuzzling my neck. His nose was warm, his tongue was wet, and well... I was lonesome.

It wasn't long before the fight broke out. You knew it was coming. So did I and everybody else. After all, there's not a single documented case of werewolf or biker having a quiet drink then going home. They live to break heads and bruise knuckles, then lick up the spilled blood.

I figured as long as I was

with Loupe, I was safe... until Big Love and Shaggy, locked in a World Federation Wrestlers' clench, crashed into our table, turning it into splinters. By the time I'd picked myself up, Loupe was gone.

Somebody threw a beer, somebody used a boot, and suddenly everybody in the bar was brawling, with the exception of the band. Fangs were bared, claws extended and a blood-cry rang through the room.

Basically, the humans were toast and dinner was served.

* * *

You can skip the occult encyclopedias, the Universal Monster Movie Marathon, and the Exterminator's Guide to Supernatural Pests if you're looking for an answer as to how we got out of there with our skins and jugulars in tact.

Rare Were and Shaggy had used steak knives to stake down three customers to the buffet tables and were arguing over who got center cut. Moonstruck and WYCCM-Jack were clawing their way through a tabletop barricade that was all that lay between them and the kitchen, where they planned to charbroil a couple of skinny kids lofted over their heads by a single paw. I thought I spotted Loupe near the band fiddling with the monitors, but I wasn't sure. The next moment, the music was blaring at about a hundred and twenty decibels, and wolf and human alike were clutching at their tender ears.

They say music can sooth the soul of a savage beast. All I know is, in a blink of an eye or the sounding of a long guitar note, the werewolves' minds turned from dinner to dancing.

The band was in the middle of the instrumental section of Lou Reed's "Sally Can't Dance ('Cause She's Dead)." Moonstruck dropped the girl he'd been carrying and dragged her toward the bandstand. The dance floor was packed by the time the rather startled and suddenly stage-petrified lead singer remembered the words to the next verse.

Fright hadn't completely petrified their frontal lobes 'cause it occurred to the band to segue without a break straight into Jim Carol's "Those are the People Who Die." It was an obscure Ramones/Velvet Underground/Punk Rock kind of song, but the wolves all knew it, and a bunch of 'em had clustered around the fourth mike by the time the band reached the chorus.

Loupe popped up at my side just then, and after I finished a shreik, I asked him what he wanted.

"You got any mousse?"

I dug in my purse, pulled out a can. He grabbed it and disappeared. Halfway through the crowd he lobbed it at Shaggy, then took off toward the bar. When he popped up again, he was carrying a bottle of red wine and two glasses. He handed those to me, righted a table and a couple of bar stools and we settled in for the show.

Shaggy emerged from the john; he'd slicked his hair back in a Duck-ass and shaved away enough hair to highlight massive sideburns. His coat collar was turned up and he looked for all the world like a leather, second-comeback, Elvis. Which was a good thing, cause King Velvet had the Vegas, sequins-and-jumpsuit period covered. Velvet made room at the mike and the two launched into a duet of "Blue Moon of Kentucky." Sure the band had already played it, but who was going to complain?

From there, they segued into "That's Alright Mama," through "Blue Suede Shoes," and out the far side to a medley of "Tutti Frutti" and "Lawdy Miss Clawdy." Somewhere in the string of songs, they'd picked up a furry quartet of back-up singers. The wolves not only sang decent four-part harmony, they had Temptations-style choreography all worked out.

The bar brawl almost resumed when the middle dancer high-kicked a little too enthusiastically, booting Shaggy in the backside. But a quick round of beers, compliments of the bar, soothed the ruffled fur.

By popular request, the band started the next set out with "When My Blue Moon Turns to Gold Again," then moved back into the classics with "Heartbreak Hotel," "Hound Dog" and an extended version of "Don't Be Cruel" (thanks to El Nino's solos and a Band Stand dance-off by the back-up singers – Rare Were won, by popular applause).

The band was running out of Elvis songs when the group wrapped things up with a tearful rendition of a young country boy who had to shoot his dog when he got old, in "Old Shep," complete with a final chorus of lonesome howls sent up by every wolf in the room.

* * *

When we stumbled out of there yawning and rubbing our smoke-filled eyes at seven the next morning, we realized the Blue Moon had set and the New Sun had rose without any bloodshed – though the bar had to pay triple price to get a case of Bloody Mary Mixer delivered at five A.M.

Loupe de do Garou was worried there might be big bad wolves lurking around who weren't so gentlemanly as him, so he walked me home, promised to call, and waited 'til I'd triple-locked the door.

Last I heard, the werewolves had joined the Mini-Reubens as back-up singers, and they'd lined up a Midwest tour under the name of Claude Raines is Sick in Bed with the Blue Moon Fever – also known as BMF, for short.

Tina L. Jens has had more than 70 short stories published, more than half of which were in mass market anthologies including: Diagnosis: Terminal (Tor/Forge); Phantoms of the Night (Daw); Shock Rock II, with Bob Weinberg. (Pocket Books); 10 anthologies edited by Martin H. Greenberg and associates (multiple publishers)

Her first novel, **The Blues Ain't Nothin': Tales of the Lonesome Blues Pub** (Design Image Group) was a final nominee for the Bram Stoker award and International Horror Guild award for best first noveo, and won the National Federation of Press Women's award and the IL Women's Press Assoc. awards for best novel.

She is the founder of Twilight Tales, Inc, a weekly reading series and small press, and served as the editor there for 9 years, publishing 26 chapbooks, collections, and anthologies in that time.

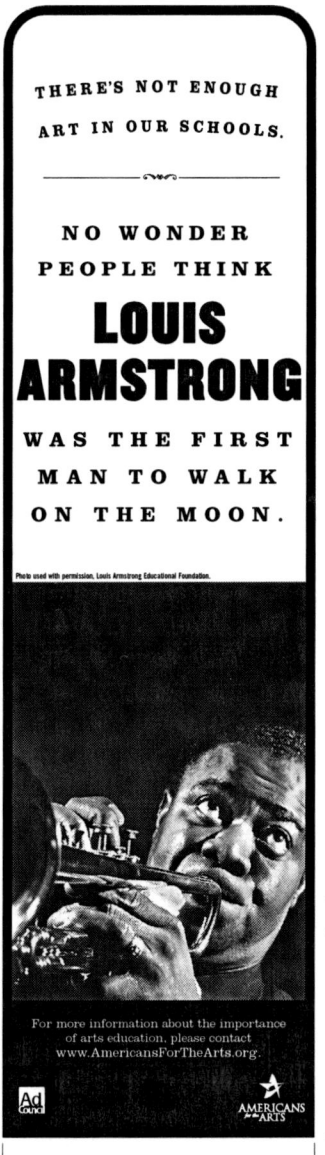

Shroud 3   The Journal of Dark Fiction and Art

Beneath The Shroud

An Interview with MICHAEL MARSHALL SMITH

By Marie O'Regan

Michael Marshall (Smith) *has established himself as a bestselling novelist in both the thriller and genre markets. As Michael Marshall Smith he is the author of the award-winning* **Only Forward, Spares** *and* **One of Us** *(both optioned for film), as well as the collections* **What You Make It** *and* **More Tomorrow**. *As Michael Marshall, he brought us* **The Straw Men, The Lonely Dead** *and* **Blood of Angels**. *Shroud spoke to Michael about his latest release, The Intruders, currently in development as a series for BBC.*

MOR: What sparked the idea for The Intruders?

MMS: What we're like, as people. The continual dualism, ever-present mild dissatisfaction and confusion over our identities... And observing, first-hand, the development process of a very small child...

MOR: It's the most overtly supernatural of the Michael Marshall novels. Again, was that a deliberate choice?

MMS: Yes and no. Again, it was the idea that drove the book - once I'd established what it was I wanted to write about, taking a step towards the more overtly supernatural was the only way to go. But then I had to consider whether this was a step I was happy taking, given the rigid genre constraints of publishing at the moment, and the apparent unwillingness of a lot of readers to enjoy a novel if it's not exactly the same kind of thing that the author produced last time. I decided I was going to take the step, for better or worse... If you're not true to the idea, the book's never going to stand a chance of being any good at all. And my next novel will take another step in that direction. The first fiction I wrote was horror, and it's a genre I feel very comfortable in, so long as I'm allowed to bring a bit of crime and thriller fiction along with it...

MOR: How did you approach the

Photo Courtesy of Steve Double

research for The Intruders?

MMS: In my usual, somewhat vague way... :-) I didn't need to do anything around the central idea, as that was right there in my head. But it was a novel that was firmly based in a particular locale - Seattle in particular and the Pacific Northwest in general. These are areas that I had some familiarity with already, but I wanted to make sure the story felt properly bedded there - so I flew out to Washington State for a week by myself (via a stopover in Santa Monica, also featured in the book, a place I like very much indeed) and spent every day walking the streets of Seattle from nine in the morning until six, then sitting in bars in the evening, making sure I felt I'd seen the place, and had a feel for it. That's the kind of research I enjoy: and I believe you can only really get to know a place by pounding its streets, over and over and round and round, seeing it from different angles and at different times and under different conditions, getting under the veneer of novelty and a little closer to the reality.

MOR: The Servants is being described as a YA novel. Was this how you saw the story when it first occurred to you?

MMS: Um, it's not, actually. It's being released, in the UK at least, as a 'literary' novel - which is how I first saw it. I very much hope it'll also be seen and read by the YA market, and the cover (art) doesn't fight against that, but I didn't write it specifically for that market - as it's not one I know a great deal about.

MOR: Is YA a direction you'd like to revisit? Or was it a by-product of the story rather than a conscious choice?

MMS: It was a product of the story, which it should always be. I'm mistrustful of writing specifically to markets, because it limits your freedom as to what you can put in a book. I also think it's very positive for young people to encounter material with adult themes and perspectives, to get these foreshadowings of the grown-up world, rather than always being shown stuff that has been tailored specifically for what older people believe their concerns and interests to be. I slogged through War and Peace when I was thirteen, and soon afterwards discovered Kingsley Amis and never looked back; partly, that just shows that I was a pretentious little bastard, of course, but I still got a great deal from being exposed to un-childlike ways of thinking and story-telling and self-expression. Naturally, there's a real place in the world for books targeted sympathetically for a younger market, but I'm personally more interested in writing stories that could appeal to all ages. The Michael Marshall novels are a little too adult for younger readers - and might well bore them to tears: but I do suspect there will be some more M. M. Smith books... When I get some time...

MOR: To what do you attribute your success?

MMS: Good fortune and bloody-mindedness, as much as anything else. My 'success' - to the limited degree I'd claim to have achieved any - is probably due to the fact that whatever I do is more-or-less what I meant to. You may not like my books, but I really do mean what I say - within the harsh constraints of talent and deadlines. I doubt I'll ever scale the heights of super-bestsellerdom, partly because of this, but I can live with that. I'm only going to write so many novels during my life. I want to make sure that none of them make me wince. You also need to remember that writing is a job, not just some ineffable art form. You have to bed down, stick with it, be willing to go toe-to-toe with fate, disappointment and publishers. All three will knock you flat nine times out of ten, but it doesn't do to let them see the fear in your eyes.

MOR: What can we expect next?

MMS: Well, there's a lot of stuff up at the moment... I'm writing a new novel - tentatively entitled Bad Things. I'm co-writing a feature adaptation of a short story of mine called Hell Hath Enlarged Herself for the UK Film Council, and co-writing (with Stephen Jones) an animated horror movie for kids called Monstermania for Uli Meyer Animation. BBC development of The Intruders is moving forward in the background, The Straw Men is being adapted to comic and graphic novel form, and just before Christmas, I completed the first draft of a TV adaptation of Mrs Todd's Shortcut, the Stephen King short story, for a possible project with Granada. So

I'm keeping off the streets...

Marie O'Regan *is a horror and dark fantasy writer based in the Midlands. She has had stories published widely in such magazines as Dusk, Dark Angel Rising, Here and Now, Midnight Street, and in anthologies like The Alsiso Project from Elastic Press, When Darkness Comes and Terror Tales, alongside Richard Christian Matheson, Simon Clark and Peter Straub. Marie is also the Chairperson of the British Fantasy Society, for which she has worked on projects involving Clive Barker, Neil Gaiman, John Connolly, Ramsey Campbell and Stephen Gallagher, and she has edited both their publications Dark Horizons and Prism in the past. Her first collection, Mirror Mere, came out in Spring 2006 to much acclaim, with authors like Muriel Gray and Kelley Armstrong calling it 'satisfyingly nasty' and 'a delicious batch of tightly written, shivers-up-the-spine chillers'. She also writes for magazines such as Dreamwatch, Dark Side, Writers' Forum, Fortean Times, Hub, Rue Morgue and Red Scream. Forthcoming from her is a new novella, film scripting work, and a full-length novel called Icon. You can visit her website at http://www.marieoregan.net.*

- -

LIMITED EDITION PICCIRILLI, ILLUSTRATED!
"ALL YOU DESPISE"
SIGNED BY TOM PICCIRILLI, BRIAN KEENE, AND ALEX MCVEY

WWW.SHROUDMAGAZINE.COM

HELP SAVE THE TABARD INN!

WITHOUT YOUR HELP, THE NEW ISSUE OF TABARD INN: TALES OF QUESTIONABLE TASTE, WILL BE THE LAST.

ORDER ISSUE THREE TODAY! PAY VIA PAYPAL AT THE WEBSITE, OR SEND A CHECK OR MONEY ORDER MADE OUT TO:

JOHN BRUNI
468 E. VALLETTE ST.
ELMHURST, IL 60126

#1 OR #2=$5+$1 S&H
#3=$12+$3 S&H
#1&2=$9+$2 S&H

ORDER ALL THREE
FOR $23!
NO SHIPPING!

ISSUE THREE IS NOW AVAILABLE AT DARK DELICACIES (DARKDEL.COM) AND HORROR-MALL.COM!

#3 IS NO MERE MAGAZINE: WITH 32 STORIES, ONE POEM, ONE RANT, AND TEN PHOTOGRAPHS, IT IS AN ANTHOLOGY. DON'T MISS IT!

TALESOFQUESTIONABLETASTE.COM

BEFRIEND TUSITALA AT MYSPACE.COM/TABARDINN

SHADOWS IN THE SNOW
Phil Kuhlman

The chill of winter fell hard across most of the territory, but the population of Oeste, Texas was spared from the white wrath of the falling snow for another year. Maybe it was due to the warm rivers running up from the gulf, maybe it was due to the location said to be lucky by local tribes. Whatever it was, the tiny town had began to flourish and grow over the last two years since its construction. However, some of the Indians had called the land lucky when they lived there; now they called it cursed. The ground ate up by the iron road, the land used up for tobacco and horses. The Indians themselves were used up too, the once great tribes of the area now all but gone. The last of the Indians who still lived near the town kept his distance, angry, but accepting of the fate that had fallen upon his once strong people and land.

Adults warned local children to stay away from "Old Leather" as they called him. They were afraid that he'd use his "ancient ways" to bring plague down on their homes. Maybe they just felt guilty over what they'd done to him and his people, and demonizing the man was easier than living with him as an equal. Whatever it was, over the years, as the city aged, and those children grew into adults, Old Leather seemed to stay just as ancient as before, only appearing in town to purchase goods, and sometimes strange things that a man living in a tiny hut wouldn't have much use for. Tiny lead balls left over from the remains of the civil war; wads and wads of old cloth; food too old for normal folk to enjoy, too old for an old Indian man to make edible with any amount of know-how or "magic", and even more strange things. Despite the strange things, Old Leather was allowed to have his way around town, people didn't disturb him, and he would rarely even look at anything but his path away from the skeleton that was now living on the land he grew up upon.

The winter changed suddenly, sharply, like the claws of an old crone across flesh, and it tore away at the reserve of the people of Oeste. Plague came next, as communication and travel was suddenly cut away by the coldest winter any of them had ever seen. They weren't prepared for snows like this, living deep inside of Texas. The warm rivers seemed to stop flowing, the lifeblood no longer surrounding the community, the sun blocked away by acres of uncaring blankets of clouds. Soon, they began to look for the cause. It was at that time that a preacher came forth with an old book carried by his family from Salem years before. The Mallaeus Malificarum. The "holy tome" stated very clearly to the people that these ill events were being caused by a malicious outsider. At first, the town rejected the idea, but as they began to starve and suffer from disease, they began to believe that God had sent down his wrath upon them.

Still, through all of this, Old Leather walked through town and back to his shack each day, picking up supplies, unhindered by the cold or the suffering around him. He had seen winters like this before. The people of the town however, hadn't. And this is what led them to believe they had found their malicious outsider. How could he have been so old, yet look the same as he had for years? How could he look so alive while the town died around him? It was these questions that would drive the town to violence.

On a night with no wind, a group of five men prepared to do their holy duty, armed with blades and clubs. No need to waste ammunition on a single old man when there was still a chance something edible may still be alive out in the wastes. It didn't take long to find him; his shack was on an area of green and brown grass, the only clear spot in the whole area. In a matter of minutes, they had broken in, but he was already aware of them. He sat, face highlighted by nothing but moonlight as he looked up from his rations into the eyes of his attackers. With a slight grin, he said something in a language the men had never heard, but the words shook the reserve of each man, sending electrical pulses through their body, screaming "Something is wrong here, we shouldn't be here," but it wasn't enough. Old Leather continued his incantation as the men drew steel and began to hack into him, stripping flesh from bone, limb from torso, leaving him nothing but a bloody pile of former humanity. Then came the looting, taking all they could bear on their backs and horses, even killing and feasting on Old Leather's horse before leaving the old shack in the lonely hollow.

The trek back home seemed longer than before. The wild winds and razor-like rains and snow seemed intent to punish the men for what they had done. Within two days, one of the men had died. Unable to bury him, they had to leave him lying near the campsite. It was that night that he came.

In the small hours of the night, the moon seemed to hide for a moment behind one of the black clouds, choking away all

light, but not sound. The crunch of snow and breaking grass grew louder as the moments in the dark continued on without a sign of ceasing. The very lack of wind implied the clouds had simply chosen to sit by and allow the men's minds tear away at their resolve. Perhaps it would have been best to stay in the dark, as what the light revealed was far worse.

There he was, the bloodied form of Old Leather mounted on his butchered horse. A grin would have been smeared across his face had he lips to use. He tossed down the dead body of the fifth member of the party, sending it rolling into the fire. The scent of burning flesh both filled the men with horror and a sick hunger. Old leather spoke again, but he didn't use his ruined mouth; his voice seemed to come from everywhere, from bush, from sand, from tree, from inside the terrified men's heads.

"Wendigo." His words were gurgled and thick, the men screamed with horror, unable to escape from the cold glare of the now obvious moon and the outline of the rotting horseman. And with that, the specter turned away, and rode back towards the shack. The moon again hid, and when it was back, the horse and rider had vanished as well, no prints, nothing. Nature's fast coat of snow also concealed evidence of the horrific apparition. All that remained was the burning odor of the fifth murderer, now the murdered. The men tried as they could to resist the sick urges now growing in them, and to fight the even worse sensations they were now dealing with. One of the men noticed that his flesh was turning black, falling off in parts. Another could no longer feel his heart beating. These feelings soon affected them all as they cowered from the horrific winds. After days of this, three of the men died, leaving only one to fight against the elements.

However, the dead didn't stay that way. Within hours, the rotting corpses were moving again, feasting on the burnt flesh of Old Leather's gift, the murderer now murdered. The sole survivor ran, and it seemed that within hours he was home. All that time lost in the wastes and they had been only hours from safety! He was welcomed by horrific screams, and word that the preacher who had pushed them all to vengeful murder was found hanging in his church the morning before. His appearance was horrific; rotted, blackened. But the people only believed this the effects of exposure.

The next day the survivor was given word that the other men had been spied traveling over the hill toward town. The messenger didn't get a chance to get back out of the room though, as sick hunger had overwhelmed the survivor, driving him to savage the young man, and feast upon his bloody, pulpy flesh. In his mind though, he tried to fight it, he was no longer in control of his body, only the beast-like hunger and urge to kill. Soon he could hear the screams outside as the returning dead began to feed as well. He screamed in his mind about what he was doing, unable to stop shoving the flesh into his mouth, feeling every hot chunk of human slide down his throat. The other men were facing this as well, the urge to kill and eat their fellow man without control of their own bodies. Within hours, there a pile of corpses littered the center of the skeletal town, the ice and snow dyed black and red from the carnage. A small stock of people hid in the basement of the old church, the screams of the remaining survivors remaining a constant dreadful reminder, but the hunger stalked them too, as did the pallid horseman with his horrific gift of sustenance.

It would be months until the snows abandoned the town, leaving behind the remains of a dead city and the signs of struggle. Blood, some bones, scraps of bodies, no full corpses. Word was that a troupe of soldiers on patrol for Indian raiders in the area came across a mad group of cannibal savages dressed in rotten human skins and carrying jerkied human flesh. In the course of the fight, the soldiers hammered them with bullets, yet none of the vile figures fell. "Madness" would be the excuse for this, but it was due to their inability to kill the madmen that caused the soldiers to fabricate a series of forts, fighting off the cannibals as well as they could until they figured out a way to wall them in. After that, the soldiers flooded the dead valley with the warm gulf river water. They returned to work at other posts, leaving the strange underwater city as nothing but a curious footnote in the history of ghost towns. Decades later, an old Indian man would come forward with the deed to the town. He asked that the remains of the people lost in the icy winter so many years ago be exhumed and given a proper burial. Divers sent for the reclamation never returned, the last place they recorded investigating was the old church, still visible from the top of the dam in the right light. Every fifty years or so, an old man would come forward with proof of ownership asking for divers to investigate the old skeleton of Oesta, always with different reasons. For science, for burial, to appraise the quality of the water, but tragedy always overcame the retrievals.

I know why though. He told me this story, showed me scars from a horrific attack, and even let me see a horse he'd had for years covered in scars and a crimson coat. He told me this tale, wearing a horrific smile the whole time. Seems he felt it was time for someone to know what happened to Oesta and what rested beneath the fresh water. There wasn't anything I could do about it. The dam was set for demolition in two days, and winter was on the way.

⸻◇◇◇◇◇⸻

Phil Kuhlman *woke up on Easter of 2006 paralyzed. After the discovery of a Lovecraftian horror hidden in his ribcage as the culprit of the attack on his spine (read: a tumor) he's been through half a year of intensive chemo and so far a full year of physical therapy. Though it impeded his ability to walk for several months, it did not stop him from writing. Now cancer free and sporting a 9* inch scar down his back, he has taken all of this in as inspiration for the field of Horror Fiction. He lives near the center of Texas in Kerrville with a 20 pound black cat named Indigo. A lifelong student of the work of Lovecraft, Matheson and King, he hopes that he can both be a credit to the cancer survivors of the world and the horror fans who have given him this chance to tell this, his first published work. More of his writing can be found at www.writerscafe.org/writers/phil kuhlman.

Malcolm McClinton

Shroud 3   The Journal of Dark Fiction and Art

A Museum Piece
by Ken Goldman

> *"Oh, they loved dearly; their souls kissed, they kissed with their eyes, they were both but one single kiss!"*
>
> —Heinrich Heine, German Poet

As field trips went, this one to the Museum of Natural History so far had proven lame. What could you really say about the breeding habits of the Alaskan sea otter that would moisten the panties of any seventeen year old school girl? The twenty St. Clotilde students concluded their tour with a visit to the popular Human Oddities wing, and finally the museum showed some promise. The girls gazed at two skulls conjoined at the jaw and preserved behind glass. The golden identification plate offered little more information than the French names belonging to the skeletal heads.

Someone asked, "Were these Siamese twins or something?"

The young tour guide's name tag read BELINDA, and she held a special place in her heart for this grotesque anomaly, especially since the past summer. On some days she kidded her younger guests that the exhibition piece had been used as a paperweight by Marilyn Manson, then quickly moved on with the tour. Today she felt like talking.

"These are the skulls of Francoise La Bourliere and her paramour Antoine Furois, Parisian sweethearts of the French aristocracy dead nearly fifty years who met their end one spring morning as they strolled along the Seine. Their story is clouded by inaccuracies and exaggeration, but I can detail a pretty faithful version. Want to hear?" Belinda had developed a respectable flair for the dramatic on this job, and her voice dropped a pitch. "Do you young ladies believe in magic?"

Most of the group nodded, but not Suzanne. Wearing a fashionable red scrunchie that offset her starched parochial school uniform, the pretty disbeliever decisively shook her head. "Magic is crap. It didn't work so well for Siegfried and Roy, did it?"

A wise assed kid. Every school group had its junior iconoclast, and kids seething with angst were Belinda's favorites. Not long ago she had been one of them. She beaded in on Suzanne.

"Then maybe you believe in passion? You see, Antoine desired Francoise from the moment he first saw her. Fearing she might not return his affection, he -"

Belinda paused to look over her shoulder. This part of her narrative could be delicate if the school's dour nuns lurked nearby. The bad little girl living inside her was alive and well. Five years out of Holy Savior and she still checked to see if the Sisters were watching.

" . . . he procured the services of a sorceress named Amelie who might encourage the young woman's favor. Although Amelie was as hideous as Francoise was beautiful, after one hour spent with the young and wealthy monsieur she determined to have him for herself."

"Did she cast a spell on him?" one grossly overweight student asked the guide. The more homely school kids usually seemed the most interested in knowing about the power of magic spells. Maybe those who were themselves different needed to believe in witchery the most.

Belinda slipped into tour-speak mode. "Even the best magic is never fool proof. But Amelie cast no spell on Antoine he hadn't selected for himself. The woman understood her blackest magic was a poor substitute for true love, and she refused using it to win Antoine's affection. Correctly intuiting matters of the heart, she offered the smitten man a vial containing a strong potion of exotic and forbidden herbs. If lovers sipped the vial's contents, she instructed, afterward the liquid allowed each of them one wish pertaining to the other."

The heavyset school girl frowned. "That wasn't very smart of the sorceress if Amelie wanted Antoine for herself."

Belinda smiled. This kid needed a few more years to grasp a clear understanding of the evil intentions of which women were capable.

"The most clever woman never lets on that she is. The sorceress believed that behind all male desire lurks a consuming need to possess. Amelie knew Antoine would desire that Francoise be his forever, and Francoise's assurance of eternal fidelity would likely become his one wish. That meant for the rest of his days the woman would cling to her lover like an itching garment. In time the sorceress knew Antoine would return to her little shop an exhausted man, begging for release from a constant lover who allowed him no rest. Amelie would offer the poor man relief, of course. He would be in her debt, and then she would have him."

This part of the story stirred memories, and the guide glanced toward the entranceway where the museum's dark-haired curator stood, Geoffrey B. Haskin, whose family had a considerable financial interest in the place. Belinda quickly looked away. She noticed the girl with the red scrunchie was watching him too, and why not? He was a real looker, there was no denying that. But Belinda's narrative was not meant for a man's ears, especially this man's.

"The next morning Antoine persuaded Francoise to meet him at a small café, the revolving Tuileries Carousel along the Seine. When a particularly beautiful swan distracted the young woman, he sipped some of the sorceress' potion, then emptied the remainder into Francoise's tea. The results were instantaneous. The longing expression in his woman's eyes encouraged the suitor to waste no time in speaking his heart. He insisted he would never leave her, adding he had but one desire - - to hear those same words from her. Smothering him with kisses, the smitten Francoise readily whispered them. And so, one wish had been uttered and granted.

"Hand in hand they walked the path along the Left Bank, each hopelessly immersed in love for the other, stopping frequently to steal a kiss along the way. The further they walked, the more passionate their kisses became.

"The potion's effects had almost expired when Antoine, hoping to benefit from the full effects of the sorceress' brew, whispered, 'My love, today you have granted me my greatest wish. If you had one wish you would ask of me, what would that be?' Francoise didn't hesitate telling him 'I wish I could go on kissing you forever!' Too overtaken with the moment, the man hadn't realized the tragic portent of his lover's desire until she pressed her parted lips to his. Their mouths immediately became one skin impossible to separate. Stealing one another's breath with every inhale, the two struggled to break free of their death kiss. Attempts to scream made matters worse. Onlookers strolling by pointed and laughed, misunderstanding what terrible thing had occurred. The lovers' end came quickly, and I suppose that was fortunate. Even in death, no one could divide them. Each had got their wish and here are their skulls to tell you about it."

Suzanne scrunched her face. "Ewwwwwwww!"

"There's a little postscript to this story, but it's kind of personal. You guys interested?"

The girls' nods were unanimous.

"Last summer following senior year in college I was nursing a broken heart of my own. I visited Paris, losing myself in walks along the Seine and sipping wine in a dozen outdoor cafés with exotic names like Deux Magots and La Coupole along the Left Bank, making my way along the Saint-Germain-Des-Pre in the fashionable district of Montparnasse. By accident I came upon a small shop run by an old woman who called herself Madame Amelie. She was even uglier than I imagined, her troll-like hideousness compounded by an extremely ungraceful old age that had transformed the woman into a hag. Waiting until the shop emptied, I approached her.

"'Francoise La Bourliere and Antoine Furois, Madame. Do you know these names?'" I asked in the poorest French ever uttered. The woman didn't bat an eye. But finally she spoke.

"'Mademoiselle, few Parisians of my years have not heard those names.' The Madame was, of course, correct. In its day the bizarre story had spread throughout France. But word of mouth had distorted the truth, and over time the tale became regarded as fiction among most clear thinking Frenchmen. Deciding to be more direct I handed the old woman a fistful of francs. After examining the money, she looked closely at me.

"'Qu'est-ce que c'est?'

"'Madame Amelie, I know the story of those doomed lovers. I know about your role in it.' I could see the woman had become agitated and required some assurance of my intentions. 'I have no reason to judge you, Madame. In fact, I'm very glad to have found you. You see, there is a matter that concerns my own heart.'

"I explained to the old woman about a young man who recently had lied to me, one day promising love and the next deciding he had tired of me. Knowing he had broken my heart, he pursued another woman before my eyes. If the sorceress' potion could salvage what remained of the man's love for me - or at least help me get over mine - I assured her I would someday return to Paris with several additional fists full of francs.

"'Men talk a fine game, Mademoiselle. They speak quite freely of forevers.' That's all she muttered before disappearing into her parlor to mix a batch of her magic. She returned within a few minutes, impatient to send me on my way. I understood why.

"I wondered if maybe I were doing the right thing, questioned whether I'd been foolish to even believe in magic or sorcery. But when I returned home I slipped the potion into the man's coffee and decided from that moment I was done with him. And, happily, I am! So maybe there is something to be said for magic, huh?"

Belinda savored the moment of triumph she had created, but a shrill voice interrupted her rumination. Another group of museum visitors stood waiting in their queue while their pissed off guide shuffled about with nothing to do. The blonde woman displayed a noticeable hobble in her step as if this job had required too much time spent on her feet.

"Let's move it, Belinda! How about wrapping it up so my group can see some of the exhibits too before closing time?"

"Sorry, Lydia. We're moving right now. Okay girls, you heard the nice lady!" A peaches and cream smile emerged, although some of the cream had gone sour. "That limp looks like it's getting pretty bad. Maybe someone should look at it."

Managing her own affected smile that displayed a complete lack of warmth, the blonde steered her group quickly past Belinda whose own smile suggested something much worse.

* * *

Suzanne had watched the mini drama unfold. It was like playing connect the dots when she had been little. Already her brain penciled in the spaces to form a picture, and the picture included three people. The good looking man in the museum appeared too well dressed for a museum worker, and he had been standing in that same spot too long to be a tourist. Suzanne had seen enough TV soapers to recognize a lovers' triangle when she spotted one, but she said nothing to her classmates. Instead, she approached her tour guide with one huge shit-eating grin as if she had solved an incredible math equation.

"That well dressed man over there. . . and that blonde tour guide? Are they--?"

Belinda winked at Suzanne in the universal language shared among all women. Suzanne watched as her guide approached the man, the girl inching closer to listen for whatever further drama unfolded. She knew this was eavesdropping, an act that would earn her sore knuckles if Sister Agatha saw. She didn't care.

"Hello, Geoffrey," Belinda said, but she pronounced it JEFF-rey as if making some kind of point.

The man said nothing.

"Something wrong? Cat got your tongue?"

Face contorted, seeming pained and confused, he managed to speak.

"Heh-wo, Beh-wij-a . . ."

It seemed he had tried to say 'Hello Belinda,' but what came out resembled nothing like that. He sounded like someone who had taken diction lessons from Elmer Fudd, his speech impediment so pronounced several St. Clotilde girls standing nearby stifled giggles. Suzanne thought that seemed cruel enough, but felt especially bewildered by her tour host's harsh greeting when she must have been aware of the poor guy's disadvantage. Suzanne would have questioned Belinda about that, but Sister Agatha wanted the girls inside the bus for the return trip to St. Clotilde's, so goodbyes were hasty. Suzanne said nothing to Belinda nor to anyone else, selecting a seat apart from the others.

Some dots refused to connect. The girl continued working events over in her head thirty minutes later as the bus entered the Interstate and her classmates had joined together in a singing pop chorus of Britney Spears crap. Something was missing, all right, something no one had detected. Suzanne rewound her mind's video of the past hour.

Lydia, the other woman.

["That limp looks like it's getting pretty bad."]

. . . and the handsome and dapper lover who could hardly speak Belinda's name as if . . .

["Cat got your tongue?"]

Something in that . . . yes, something only Belinda knew.

[The most clever woman never lets on that she is.]

. . . and maybe there is something to be said for magic.

What had Belinda said were Francoise's last words to Antoine?

"I wish I could go on kissing you forever . . ."

[Forever . . .]

Something else . . . something else from Amelie the hag . . .

"Men talk a fine game, Mademoiselle. They speak quite freely of forevers."

Talk . . .

Hello, JEFF-rey. Cat got your tongue?

["Heh-wo, Beh-wij-a . . ."]

. . . Kiss . . . Tongue . . .

French kissing . . . or something else? Something . . .

. . . dirtier?

[Cat got your tongue?]

Cat . . . kitten . . . puss-puss . . .

Puss-Puss got your tongue . . .???

Suzanne bolted forward in her seat. While the school bus filled with song, in her mind's eye the young and handsome man was kissing blonde Lydia, all right. But not on her lips, oh no, not on her lips at all, but somewhere else. . . somewhere else where the cat had gotten his tongue. And kept it too!

. . . down there!!!

[Forever!]

["That limp looks like it's getting pretty bad."]

Suzanne's face contorted with disgust. Nearby her schoolmates stopped singing and

turned to stare when she squealed.

"Ewwwwwwwwwwwwwwwww . . . ."

◇◇◇◇◇

Ken Goldman *has previously been a high school English and Film Studies teacher (Horror and Science Fiction in Film and Literature) at George Washington High School in Philadelphia, Pennsylvania. He is a member of the former GWA, the Genre Writers Association and an Affiliate Member of HWA, the Horror Writers Association. Ken has published more than 465 stories in the small/independent press since 1993.*

THE FOWLER'S DAUGHTER
BY MICHELLE MUENZLER

It was one of those autumn days, late in the season, where the scent of wood-smoke clung to the air like a drowning man. The dry meadow grasses crackled beneath the long stride of my boots, and the cold iron of my dad's shotgun bit through the layered flannels that had also once been his. I'd flushed two pheasants in the far meadow, and now the strung-together pair swished against my back in a halting rhythm.

At the fence, I slipped through an old break. Its wood had been strong once. When I was a little girl, I had clambered along its length and pretended to fly. But that was a different me, a different fence. Given enough time, everything falls apart.

Like my dad, for instance.

I cleared the last hillock, bringing our shack and the pond into view.

"Damnit." My curse startled some quail into flight.

In the brown waters of the pond, my dad was sunk to his waist, floundering after the geese. They cackled and hissed and led him deeper. I slid the gun from my shoulder and set it in the grass along with the pheasants.

"Out of the water, Dad!" I called, hastening toward him.

His slow spiral inward continued. I gritted my teeth, splashed into the icy water, and dragged him ashore; all the while, a furious itching pricked my calves.

"Where is she?" he asked, his

voice the high-pitched whisper of a child. He shivered in my hands.

"Not here." Never here. At least not when we wanted her.

I pulled a handkerchief from my pocket, wiped the blood spittle from the corner of his blue-gray lips, and carried him home. A change of clothes and a triple layer of quilts soon quieted his shakes.

"I'll be back," I said.

His eyes proved he was already gone, lost in old memories. Did he ever dream of me, or had the geese taken even that? I trudged to my fallen catch in the meadow, a light wind pricking my cheeks and warning of colder days to come. As I bent to retrieve the pheasants, a sudden itch crinkling deep in my spine. I turned to the northern horizon. There, a dark wedge of geese pierced the blue glass of the sky like a bullet.

Mother was coming home.

* * *

I cleaned the pheasants and dropped them into a pot of yesterday's broth. Over the long afternoon, they disintegrated, flesh splitting from bone, and filled the shack with their fatty aroma. When only a sliver of the sun remained on the horizon, I left my dad wrapped in quilts and marched to the pond's edge, an old dress clenched between my fingers. Mother was waiting, swimming in quiet circles.

She changed as the last rays of red slipped away, her feathers falling into gold-flecked dust, her skin stretching toward the sky. Human again, if you could call her that.

She struggled to her feet, unsteady, and wiped the mud from her knees. "I am home."

Her voice always startled me at first, too quiet for my memory of it, and too soft for the hard angles of her face. I squeezed the dress until my fingers burned.

"Where's your father?" she asked.

"Sick." He was more than just sick this time, though.

"Then I must see him."

I pulled the dress against my stomach. "It'd be better if you didn't."

She touched my cheek, and a deep itch fluttered in my shoulder blades. I jerked away and shoved the dress into her hands.

"Don't touch me."

"I am your mother." A shadow flitted across her brow.

"In blood alone."

She stared, her goose-dark eyes unreadable, then pulled the dress over her head, and disappeared into the shack. I collected an old quilt from the porch and huddled near the pond to wait for dawn. Whenever the wind bit too hard, I tossed stones at the dozing geese. If I could have no rest, neither could they.

* * *

In the gray hour before dawn, Mother emerged, her face tight and pale. I rose from the grass, quilt still drawn tight around my shoulders. A wet hollow marked where I'd sat the night through.

"Satisfied now?" I refused to soften the bitterness in my voice. She'd kill him with her leaving.

"I will come for you in the spring."

After your dad is dead, she didn't say.

"I won't be here. I'm selling the land and moving to the city. There's already a developer lined up."

Her eyes were quiet, but the trembling of her chin told me my barb had struck. She pulled the dress overhead, folded it carefully, and handed it to me. With her eyes on the eastern horizon, she stepped into the pond. I hated her stillness on the edge of change, her calm acceptance. I hated how easily she could let her humanity slide away, like the sloughing off of dead skin.

I hated how easily she could leave us every time.

"Wait," I said, almost biting my tongue. Why should I have to speak if she would not? "You could stay. Until the end at least. Maybe I'd feel differently then." Or maybe she would remember what it was to love her family more than a flock of birds.

"They wouldn't stay," she said. "The dream of south is too strong."

"Then let them go."

She did not turn to me, and I almost lost her words as the first raw edge of dawn broke.

"I also dream."

In a glittering rain of dust, she faded. Only the goose remained.

* * *

I expected the geese to fly at any moment, and I could see they expected it as well, but she kept them there. They circled the pond restlessly and wandered the meadow with their eyes glued skyward. My dad hid himself the full day, leaving only a brittle shell for me to watch over. His open eyes reflected nothing. When the sun bled into the horizon, the geese were still there. I hurried to the shore where mother was waiting.

"You stayed," I said, handing her the dress.

"Yes." She pulled it on.

I clasped her hand, ignoring the deep itch shivering beneath my skin, and we walked together toward the shack. My chest was buoyant with giddiness. I could've flown right then.

"I'll make you a warm place by Dad's side tomorrow and make sure you're well-fed and safe during the day. No fox will make it within a thousand feet."

I glanced over, saw the shadows darkening in her eyes, and stopped.

"You're not staying, are you?"

"The south still calls. You will understand. In the spring."

She ran her free hand down my arm. I could almost feel the sickening pop of feathers bursting in her wake.

"No." I pulled myself free and stepped back. "I will never understand."

* * *

By dawn, I had settled at the pond's edge, shotgun in hand. Mother appeared, shook her head at the gun, and removed her dress, holding it out for me to take, but

I refused. Carefully, she set it in the grass.

"Spring," she said. "Wait for me."

Hadn't I waited long enough already? I wanted to ask her, but the words wouldn't come.

She slid into the water with ease and with the breaking of dawn became the goose again. Ripples fled across the pond, and her flock called out for reassurance against the tang of iron in the air.

"Stay," I said, aiming at the nervous geese. For their lives, surely she would stay.

She circled a moment in silence, then honked, and all the geese but her burst into the air. I pulled the trigger, and lead shot sprayed the scattering flock. Three of them plummeted back into the water.

They were just geese, I told myself. Nothing less, nothing more. Even Mother, black and gray and full of spite like any common goose, was no different. I aimed the rifle at her.

"Stay."

She glared; she hissed. She flapped her wings and hurtled toward the sky.

I fired.

Just geese, nothing more, I repeated again and again as her body drifted in quiet circles. Between my shoulder blades, a deep itch fluttered and pressed for freedom.

I pictured the city until it passed.

∞∞∞

Michele Muenzler's *fiction can be found in Behind the Wainscot, and is forthcoming in Electric Velocipede, Coyote Wild, and Renard's Menagerie.*

Shroud 3 The Journal of Dark Fiction and Art

Your Horror Collection Would be in Ruins without Shroud.

Visit Us Today

www.shroudmagazine.com

Books, Magazines, More

Old School Ties

Joseph D'Lacey

Still panting with the effort of carrying the warm, limp bodies through the hatch, Monty regarded the scene in the converted wine cellar with mild disbelief. Bare light bulbs hung from grey flex stapled into the damp mortar between vaulted bricks. He wiped a trickle of acidic sweat from his eye, shook his head in the forty-watt gloom.

"Fuck a duck," he said.

It had all been far too easy.

The cellar had a central walkway and eight deep recesses – four to each side. He'd replaced the wine racks with frames of sturdy wooden planks and benches on steel brackets bolted deep into the walls. Along the boards, at regular intervals, were brass clothes hooks. The network of carpentry and metalwork lining the cellar walls extended into six of the eight alcoves. He used the other two for storage.

The cellar smelled of perspiration-soaked garments. He'd installed a treadmill and spent months running on it so that he could leave soiled sweatshirts and socks lying around. It helped to create the right air. He could almost hear the hubbub of studded footsteps along corridors and the shouts of boys on their way to rugby matches.

He remembered night-time sounds, too. Sounds unheard by all but a few.

Because of the treadmill, he was a fit man, something he never dreamed he'd be. That stung. It wasn't what he wanted. None of this was what he wanted. His was a life wasted on catching up, recapturing normalcy. He could have been so many other things. Aunt Agatha would have wanted better for him. She'd lectured him on the station platform the day she packed him off to school.

"You're a man now, Saffron. You only get one life and you have to make the best of it."

Then she'd held him tight against her corseted, zeppelin bust and kissed him on the lips. Her urgent, fretful hands had pushed him up the two steps onto the train.

Slamming doors.

Harsh whistles and strangers' faces.

He had a label around his neck so that he'd arrive safely. He was seven years old.

Too young to be a man.

* * *

Things went wrong for the young Monty – Saffron Montague, as he was then – long before he went to school. His parents, who had always planned to send him to the local day school, died in a car accident when he was five years old. He and his parents' money went to his mother's already wealthy sister, Agatha.

She had grand plans for him.

She picked out two private boarding establishments: Jericho Lodge Preparatory School for his younger years and Morton College, a remote public school that would provide a classical education and advance him through the 'old boy' network.

Before the time came to send him away, she did her best to mother him. At night, terrified by solitude and the emptiness of her enormous country house, Saffron often took his cuddle-worn teddy and crawled into Aunt Agatha's bed. Equally alone, she held him close to her fallow, spinster's breasts. Hugged him a little too fondly, perhaps, as she caressed her unloved folds with surreptitious fingers.

* * *

Donald Katchurian, Toby Stokes, Wilford Holmes, Darius Wrench, Merrick Rodgers and Simon Theophilus. Names entered in pencil in a small, red notebook, indelibly in his mind.

Monty took his time arranging each man between the boards and clothes hooks, bound them tight, stopped up their mouths as they had his. Their blindfolds were the very ones they'd used on him. The positions he'd devised were more stressful than the spread-eagle or toe-touch they'd enforced – he'd had years to create them. He ensured bones made contact with hard edges, used asymmetrical attitudes to strain large muscle groups. He lashed individual fingers and toes, stretching them in unnatural planes. He organised his instruments on a surgical trolley in the central walkway of the cellar. They'd be in plain view at the moment of unveiling.

The rest of it, he'd found impossible to foresee. He couldn't hold the images in his imagination. Accordingly, he prepared for all eventualities. His were the tools of car maintenance, of oral surgery, of the Ann Summers catalogue, of horticulture and agriculture, of the health spa and massage parlour, of DIY, of the kitchen and bathroom. Some items required mains power, others were battery operated. Most just needed a little elbow grease.

There had to be pain and pleasure, as there had been for him, but it had to be better.

And much, much worse.

* * *

Most academic subjects were the same in private school as they were in those provided by the state. However, there was more on offer to those who paid for education. Saffron Montague discovered a hidden curriculum.

At Jericho Lodge Preparatory School, tutored by the brats of the gentry and the sons of the wealthy, Saffron Montague learned survival. This enabled him to reach the age of thirteen and move up a school.

At Morton College, in secret, he studied insomnia.

Some nights they came for him, others they did not. The dread kept him awake. They'd wait until 3am; when police make their raids. Everyone else in first dorm was in their deepest sleep. In the darkness he would hear the padding of slippered footsteps approaching, the rapid expectant breathing. Then they were upon him; a group of older boys, their faces hidden by balaclavas but their pyjamas not hiding their arousal.

Shroud 3 The Journal of Dark Fiction and Art

He'd feel the penknife blade cold against his throat, enough to stop him crying out for help. They would take his arms – push the blade a little deeper if he resisted – and walk him from the safety of the dorm to the other side of Rook House.

Pegs and benches lined the changing (locker) room. It smelled of turf and exertion. They were experts with the Rook House necktie, the motif of which was a black castle turret machined onto a red background in cheap, washable polyester. They used the ties to gag him, blindfold him and bind him to the changing room racks. His hooded abductors teased him erect and milked him against his will. They noosed his genitals with ties, whipped him with ties, half choked him with ties, wiped themselves off on ties before throwing the proud colours of Rook House into the communal laundry bins.

They persisted until an aspect of him waited for their arrival each night, his dread as breathless as their anticipation. They diverted Saffron Montague from the man he might have become, changed him into 'Monty'.

One night, bruised and exhausted, he'd crept back out to the laundry bins and checked the labels sewn into the backs of the soiled ties.

* * *

Monty wrote their names in a small red diary and locked it in his tuck box. A plan rooted and branched in his mind. It came to him in snatches in the middle of the night, the times they'd picked to harm him.

As suddenly as the kidnaps had begun, they ceased. The six boys in his diary were school-leavers; gone on to university and the rest of their lives. At the start of a new term, Monty waited for the blade and domination, the bondage, the pleasure and pain. He knew it would not return. Fearing it and missing it in equal measure, he never slept well again.

* * *

Monty discovered he wasn't without intelligence and worth. They'd only damaged part of him. Despite his lack of prowess on the sports field, Monty was a formidable student. By the time he left school, he'd realised the only thing stopping him from carrying out his plan was money. Earning the money, would leave no time for preparation and execution.
He needed help from Aunt Agatha.

* * *

Monty never understood why only fat women loved him, but he did his best to accept it.

Over the years there had been several. Some lasted a night or two, others became relationships. Georgina was the first. He was fifteen and at a Pagan Metal gig during Easter break. The venue was an old cinema with all the seats ripped out. A few hundred people rocked and shouted beneath cheap multicoloured lights flashing to the drumbeats in the dim hall. The band was loud and awful. He couldn't hear the words, and the feedback made his ears hurt.

But the noise and the darkness and the smell of the crowd affected him. He was anonymous among them. Entranced by the whine and clash of distorted guitar and amped drums, he turned and saw a girl beside him. She had long dark hair, witchlike in the gaudy lights, and her face was ruddy. She was six inches taller than he was and twice his width, breasts like cushions beneath green cashmere. She seemed like a woman. Mesmerised, insane, he approached her, leaned close and put his arm around her waist. She didn't stop him. He breathed her scent – sweat…and perfume.

He only held her to start with, as tenderly as he would Aunt Agatha. He pressed his cheek to her bosom. When he looked up, she kissed him. His first kiss. The boys had bitten him many times but had never kissed him. Slack-mouthed, stiff-tongued, head bursting with noise and discovery, he fell in love with the ugliest girl at the concert. It didn't matter. This was how it was meant to be – never mind that she was dreadful, never mind that she was fat. This was what had been missing.

But Monty's sexuality had already developed in ways she would never understand. He'd been brought to orgasm at the hands of abusers, been forced to mouth and sodomise them at knifepoint. He had ideas about what he wanted from the girl, but he was years ahead of her. One hand cupped the rolls of her waist, felt the muzzy softness of her flesh through the delicate wool. The other crept between her buttocks. Whereupon the girl forcefully removed it, slapped him and left the concert.

Even though he never saw her again, she became the platform for new sexual fantasies.

* * *

During the holidays, there were parties, and other fat girls who noticed him. He tried to show them his way, but it was difficult. He was so advanced that hiding his desires was impossible. One-night stands had to become longer-lived in order for him to find out how far the girls were willing to go.

* * *

His relationship with Aunt Agatha disturbed and embarrassed him. It was another chapter in a history that he didn't want. As soon as he experienced sex with females his own age, he realised what a despicable old woman she'd been. He wanted rid of her, and yet now, he fantasised about her. At night, during the holidays, he wanted nothing more than to go to her bed. He couldn't of course because she would know he was knowledgeable. He wouldn't be able to hide his interest when she squeezed him tight and caressed herself. He really was a man now, not a pipsqueak with a peanut for an erection. Yet, his masturbations left him empty and unfulfilled.

There had to be a way. And when he'd had his way, Aunt Agatha had to go.

Drugs were the answer, and they were easy to obtain. Once a week, for the rest of every holiday from school and university, Monty made sure Agatha took a heavy dose in her gin and tonic nightcap. An hour after she was in bed, barely conscious and without the strength to move her own limbs, Monty would enter her bedroom and pull back her duvet.

Arranging her corpulent body to suit himself wasn't easy, but he became adept at it over the months. The best part was being able to take his time, even say things to her or hurt her a little, knowing she wouldn't remember any of it the next day. He made her undignified, his jezebel bitch. And in the morning she became a doughy frump once more.

The game became tiring. A bore. Agatha's time approached.

* * *

'Wilf' Holmes was the first to regain consciousness.

The bone of his left shin took much of his weight., strapped at an angle to the edge of a bench. He shifted his body one way and then another, finding every direction a dead end. Through his gag, he made puzzled noises of irritation and discomfort.

Monty, dressed in pyjamas and a balaclava, removed Wilf's blindfold long enough for him to see the array of tools and the condition of his five accomplices from years before. Monty reapplied the blindfold quickly; the imagination worked better in darkness. Wilf's mind would expand and extend its snapshot of the cellar into a very personal nightmare.

He gave Wilf a playful slap on the buttock. The man went rigid with shock and then relaxed. Monty noticed a lengthening between his captive's legs, the beginnings of a beat.

Perhaps he thinks this is a game. Perhaps he thinks he'll enjoy it.

He will.

For a while.

* * *

The obituary in the local paper said Agatha Elizabeth Beaumont had died peacefully in her sleep at home. Monty was happy to see the media maintaining their tradition of printing utter nonsense. Still, they were only going on the information of the local coroner. Monty knew the inheritance due him might raise suspicion, so he made sure he received the news of her death whilst away at university. He knew her habits so well that poisoning her had been a simple matter of preparation.

He arranged a modest burial and kept the rest of her fortune for his plan.

* * *

Despite the cool air of the cellar, the six men sweated.

Each had seen. Each could imagine.

Monty strode around deciding who was first and with what. He'd heard of a technique used in IVF clinics for men whose problems were more fundamental than a poor sperm count. Monty wanted to try his own version.

Wilf had been awake longest. He would be the one.

Very much aroused himself, Monty selected the aqueous gel and cattle prod. He made sure the prod was switched off. With his victim sufficiently lubricated by an exploratory finger, he inserted the business end of the prod a couple of inches and angled it downward against his chestnut sized objective. Wilf appeared to enjoy the attention.

Monty flicked the switch.

Wilford Holmes screamed,-- loudly considering the gag--and ejaculated spontaneously all over the bench.

Monty turned the prod off, and Wilf's body collapsed as far as his restraints allowed. The cellar was silent but for the sound of men breathing harsh and tight.

Amazing, thought Monty, looking at the cooling fluid on the new wood.

He flicked the switch again and was just as astonished when a similar amount of juice jetted from his shrieking victim.

"Fuck a duck."

* * *

Monty took his time, remembering what they'd done to him. He gave pleasure. He took it away. He gave pain and made it stay.

He had a penchant for the DIY tools. The angle grinder obliterated Donald Katchurian's crotch and was unusable thereafter. Darius Wrench's scrotum was the piñata to Monty's cordless masonry drill. After all the years of waiting, the one part of the plan he hadn't been able to see in his mind was exactly what he would do to the gang that had twisted him, altered his course. Now he knew. One by one, he unsexed them, transformed their oysters to pulp. The cellar became pressurised by howls that began long before he touched them. As time passed, their voices became hoarse and their entreaties mindless.

Flicking a morsel of testicular meat from his pyjamas, Monty discovered he was no longer aroused by or interested in what he was doing. Suddenly, the men meant nothing to him. What they had done to him no longer hurt. He had forgiven them. He was purged of their sickness.

He tested himself, fantasised about men restraining him, pleasuring him, hurting him. No response. He thought about a fat girl who'd once caused him to faint at orgasm. The memory had no effect. What he wanted, he realised, was a tall, trim woman with a small waist and firm apple breasts. What he wanted was a wife and children. He wanted a car and a house and an ordinary job. The need for retribution and grotesquery was gone. He was normal.

Simultaneously, the undulating rampant rabbit in his right hand and the paint stripper in his left fell to the ground. He felt a tremendous lightness at the very core of himself. This was the way he should always have been. Here was Saffron Montague about to board the train again.

"You only get one life and you have to make the best of it."

He took the cellar stairs three at a time and burst through the heavy trap door at the top. It dropped shut with a weighty clang. The soundproofing ensured he could no longer hear the demented whines for mercy. Around him, the ruins of the farmhouse were squat and spectral in the gloaming. On the wind came the distant sound of lambs calling for their mothers. Half a mile of overgrown footpath brought him to his car. A couple of miles of broken, unused track took him to a gated road that wasn't on any map.

This is where I start from, he thought, from nowhere.

∞∞∞∞∞

Joseph D' Lacey *has had over twenty short fiction sales. This year he signed two publishing contracts for full-length work. His dystopian horror novel Meat hit UK shelves in Feb '08 with a £50,000 marketing campaign behind it. German translation rights sold to Random House/Heyne.*

ANGEL, RAPE, WHEELCHAIR
ROBERT DAVIES

The sky is the color of television tuned to his favorite porno (the living room darkened, the bottle of vodka empty, the VHS protagonists—a farmer with a harelip; his shy, myopic wife; an underfed, though eager, horse). The blue bleeds to black, and the wind is predatory, reaching into his damp sweater with icy claws. Humbert Jenkins leans down, clamps his teeth onto the spit-slickened joystick that controls his Invacare Nutron R51 motorized wheelchair, maneuvering his way closer to the red blue, red blue of the police cars and the glorious yellow streamers of "Do Not Cross" lines hanging from spindly, bare branches, and the mounded white sheet only starting to become stained.

With his thick, scabrous tongue, Humbert worries at a bit of gristle stuck between two teeth, from that most rarefied of steaks only he is able to procure.

He burps a bubble of salty blood.

A detective in perfect clothes with a perfect tan approaches, flips open his Moleskine note pad, fumbling in the pocket of his perfect coat for a shiny, perfect pen. "Excuse me, uh, sir?" he says. "You, er, didn't happen to see anything, did you?"

Humbert doesn't even bother to grunt. Amyotrophic Lateral Sclerosis (ALS). He only leers at the detective with wide, rolling eyes. For effect, he lets a thick gobbet of pink spit worm its way from the corner of his mouth. For added effect, he shits his pants, a good cup or two of wet stew. The detective's delicious partner comes up, wrinkles her nose, and pulls the perfect detective away. "We found another one in the bushes."

Oh, yes, thinks Humbert. The other steak. The two stumps that had once been his lithe, muscular legs twitch with barely repressed glee. The leprous patch that was his manhood swells pitifully. He clamps his sharpened teeth on the joystick and steers his way through the park, careful not to soil the chair's wheels with dogshit. There are standards he has to maintain. The biting winds urge him on, teasing pain from his normally numb fingertips.

He crosses the street against the traffic, causing cars to slam on their brakes, filling the air with furious honks. He tenses, praying for the cataclysm of metal on metal. He whistles Coltrane's "My Favorite Things."

As Humbert makes his way up the handicapped ramp (Handicapable, he thinks, grinning), he wonders who will clean him this time, his angel or his demon? He will let the two argue about it while he replays the feasting again and again in his mind. How for a brief moment he had loped, wolf-like among the sheep. How he had supped. The sheer joy of it!

* * *

The angel, winged and aloof, stands against the far wall, watching. Patient, as a predator must be. Gravity pulls harshly on the thin hollow bones and loose drapes of her feathered-skin. She looks pained to be standing so, grounded; her wings itch for the endless expanse of flight. There is a definite beauty in her avian face, a grace born of un-guessable ages. Tiny sparrow bones prop open her eyelids, her eyeballs dried and rheumy.

"I really don't think we have an option here, Thraxis," she says.

The demon Thraxis nods, its fur glimmering like the pelt of the perfect beast. It is massive, filling nearly half the room, fatted on the minty veal of seraphim and small boys. Great ropes of spittle hang from its mouth, its few remaining teeth cracked or broken on the spines of saints. A fat black tongue uncoils. Where wings once hung in majesty from its shoulders, there juts two small fists of bone capped with iron spikes grimed with celestial gore. On the pale flesh showing beneath its fur, scars where bones and organs have been removed flush; so cruel and wanton were the cuts, the puckered skin resembles the wobbling leers of jesters, the split-faced grins of madmen impaled on wooden spikes.

Its eyes are not the red of blood drying to black, but the warm, roseate hue of angel's sweat.

"You are right, poppet. The crip has been stringing us along."

"I propose we withhold our, ah, favors until he comes to a decision."

"Agreed," the demon says, wiping a tear of acid from his eye. "Maybe then we can get out of this dreary realm."

"No," Humbert says. "This is not the arrangement. I was told that it was up to me whether I entered Heaven or Hell. I haven't made up my mind yet."

"You have said that several times before, Mr. Jenkins. I am afraid it will no longer do."

"Bitch is right. We have superiors to answer to, you know. I have until the end of the week to acquire your soul or I'm being relieved."

"I don't even have that long, Mr. Jenkins. A Seraphim will take over just after matins." The angel purses her perfect lips. "That is unless…" She raises an eyebrow, hopeful.

"One last time," Humbert says. "I just need to do it one more time. Then I'll know."

The angel and the demon exchange knowing glances. They have heard this story many times before.

"Very well, Mr. Jenkins. But we can only give you an hour this time."

Humbert nods.

He tongues his chair from the

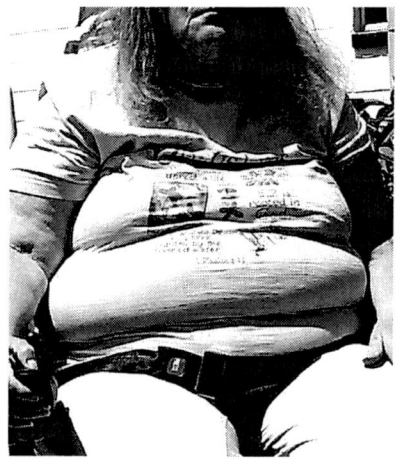

room.

The angel and the demon look at each other.

"Whose turn is it?"

The angel sighs, dropping to her knees.

The demon grins and shuffles forward.

"You better warn me," she says, opening her mouth wide.

A deep chuckle rises in the demon's hellish throat.

* * *

Humbert tongues his chair down the street and into the park, following the edges of the water.

He ignores the joggers and passing couples. They smell so sterile, so plain. The tang of youth urges him on and he forces his wheels to carry him up the hill. From the top of the hill, he can see the playground, can see the children. He rocks his chair back and forth, its motor whining, letting the desire rise in him like an unchecked fire, until it threatens to consume him with its rage. He pushes forward and coasts down the hill, biting his lip and unleashing the changing spell the immortals have given him; his wheels speed, air thrums through the spokes, and at last, as he reaches the bottom of the hill, he leaps, thrashing and silent, wild, hungry, and ever so alive. Blood glistens as it hangs in the air, red and scintillating. Skin tastes so innocent, so meaty. Perfect steel slices through muscle and sinew. Perfect steel grates on bone with a sexy whine.

He screams with delight.

* * *

"You had more than enough time to make a decision, Mr. Jenkins. Now, unfortunately, it will have to be made for you."

"This isn't what I agreed to."

The Archdaemon Umbilicus grins, baring his blood-stained fangs, and the dance of the shiny beetles across his scarred back stop for a moment. "Mr. Jenkins, you can't kick the hornet's nest over and over and then complain about getting stung."

The brilliantine glow that was Uriel's Sister speaks in flame. "It is agreed then. Shall heaven or hell administer the judgment?" The wallpaper peels from the heat.

The Archdaemon coughs out a cloud of moist flies. "It was your idea. You do it."

"You will become one of us, Mr. Jenkins," sayeth the flame. "An immortal power. You will guide mortals to their choice in time. Show them the paths available."

Humbert smiles.

The Archdaemon raises a jagged finger. "Not so fast, Mr. Jenkins. You still need a bit of seasoning before you earn your wings. Oh, I would say another lifetime. Perhaps two."

The imperishable flame grew bright, and the Archdaemon laughs.

The light that could only be the rays of salvation grow brighter and more terrible and louder, reeking of silver, and wet Paris streets before the coming of the sun, and there is night and pain and bliss and colors, so many colors, and then it is done.

Humbert slips down into the maelstrom and through it into the bloody darkness, and on into the warmth. The smell of damp hay and wet horse hair assails him. Infantile, Humbert shivers. He wails. He looks up into a hare-lipped sneer, tobacco juices staining tight lips. Beside the man is a woman. Her myopic eyes blink down at him, and she coos. A gold cross on a chain dangles between her fishbelly breasts, and it is shiny, shiny, shiny.

A horse whinnies.

◇◇◇◇◇

Rob Davies *writes stories about exploding suns, voracious babies, and crippled angels. He lives in Somerville, Massachusetts, with his wife Sara, two cats Lilith and Tiamat, and a lot of books. He has seven toes. His favorite Horseman is Pestilence. When not writing, he searches for the ideal glass of IPA and the perfect jambalaya recipe. He attended Viable Paradise, took writing workshops with James Gunn and Harlan Ellison, and sat in a doctor's office with Jack Klugman. His stories have appeared/will appear in Interzone and Weird Tales.*

AN INTERVIEW WITH EDITOR WILLIAM JONES

BY JEFF EDWARDS

William Jones is probably best known as the editor of Dark Wisdom magazine, and as the driving force behind anthologies such as Horrors Beyond 2 and Frontier Cthulhu. Recently, William took time out of his busy schedule to answer some questions about his writing, editing, and contributions to the role-playing industry.

Jeff Edwards [JE] You are involved in so many different (yet related) pursuits: fiction writing, non-fiction writing, editing magazines and anthologies, role-playing game (RPG) work, convention appearances, mentoring for the Horror Writers Association (HWA) – and the list goes on. How do you balance the things that you do?

William Jones [WJ] I'm not sure that I do balance them – at least, not as well as I once did. It seems the best planning or time management is usually thwarted by unexpected events. And, over time, the projects have increased, as have the scope of the projects. I'm trying to reduce the number of my involvements in the coming year, and hopefully find more time for each.

[JE] What are some of the challenges you face while trying to "do it all"? Surely, you must worry sometimes that the work will suffer when you're trying to do so much concurrently.

[WJ] Tackling too many pursuits can harm some or all. It is doubtful I'll ever allow myself too much free time. But having too much to do always carries the risk of reducing attention given to other pursuits. Giving proper attention to each project is more important to me than the total number of projects, and there is always the fear that one thing might suffer at the cost of another.

[JE] Do you prefer to wear the hat of writer or editor? And, as an editor, do you find that there is a bias either for or against your own fiction when you submit it to other editors?

[WJ] For me, writing and editing are deeply connected. Most of my anthology themes come from the perspective of what a writer could do with the subject. As far as seeing any bias, all of the editors I've worked with have been very professional, so I don't think it has been an issue.

[JE] Along with author David Conyers, you have parlayed an interest in the Call of Cthulhu RPG into a mutually-beneficial relationship with Chaosium, Inc. Describe the events that led to your involvement with RPG campaign-writing and sourcebooks.

[WJ] In the last century, I used to write gaming supplements for RPGs, and I also wrote fiction. Because of the nature of the hobby industry, most of the older companies have vanished. Some vanished, then reappeared, then vanished again. It wasn't until 2003 that I submitted a proposal to Chaosium for a 1920s New York City sourcebook. During that time I'd still been writing fiction – and had an ongoing series of stories set in 1920s/30s New York City. The overlapping wasn't intentional. I had plenty of information about the period, and wrote several stories in that setting. Given the publishing industry, the fiction was published long before the gaming supplement.

[JE] You edit anthologies for your own publishing house, Elder Signs Press, as well as for Chaosium. Why work with Chaosium when you have your own press? Is it for increased exposure, a sense of legitimacy by avoiding the misperception of "self-publishing" your own projects, or for other reasons?

[WJ] I more or less stumbled into publishing – it was a side effect of writing RPG books. As things progressed, Elder Signs Press became a larger undertaking, and more than a hobby. Still, I enjoy writing fiction and I have far too many strange anthology ideas for any one publisher to produce. Likewise, there are very clever ideas for anthologies out there, so I often write for them. Being a "writer/editor," I'll always work with other publishers. Similarly, I move between different genres. I write in young adult (YA), horror, mystery, science fiction, fantasy, and that elusive "dark fiction" genre. Maybe I need to be restrained.

[JE] In your fiction-writing, you are developing some "series" in the form of recurring characters such as Myron Poe, Caley Faith Dayton, and Rudolph Pearson. Why do this? Is it easier to return to a familiar character in your writing? Does it help you in a "marketing" sense, to have a body of work linked together via a central character?

[WJ] A clever question, and I wish I had a strong answer. Mainly, I'm attracted to the character or the setting or both. Many of my short fiction works play off each other. While each story is standalone, I tend to reference something in another story to connect them, as though to create an overall fictive universe. With my YA tales, I simply continued the characters' stories because it seemed there was more to be told. And with Rudolph Pearson, I was playing off the supernatural detective genre, so he was a natural to repeat. But I'm not sure that it is easier to return to the characters. Each has his or her own narrative style, and there are many facts that need to be reviewed when writing an on-going story. Other than returning to "old friends," I think creating new stories is probably easier. As for the marketing aspect, I'm not sure if it works better or not. I haven't put much thought into that factor yet.

[JE] Your book, The Strange Cases of Rudolph Pearson, was released by Chaosium in April 2008. Let's talk more about the character. Pearson is a professor of Medieval Studies at Columbia University in the early 1900s. Is there anything more you can tell us about him? What sort of trouble does he get himself into?

[WJ] Rudolph Pearson is a character thrown into a world of shadows. But he sees what goes unnoticed by others. In a sense, he lifts the shroud of reality – finding the things that have always been lurking in the dark places of the world. The Pearson character and stories are a blend of Lovecraftian Mythos and Urban Fantasy. That combination leaves plenty of room for "trouble." He is not an "investigator" of the supernatural so much as he is a man who has looked into the abyss and cannot turn away from its secrets.

[JE] Pearson has been making appearances for some time, first in magazines, then in a chapbook from Naked Snake Press. Is it rewarding to be able to collect the tales in one place?

[WJ] Yes, very much so. One, it keeps me from having to point to several books and magazines for those who want to read all of the Pearson tales. And it allows me to expand upon the character.

[JE] Are all of the stories in the volume reprints, or is there new work as well? Did you go back and revise the older work, or are the existing stories being presented in their original form?

[WJ] There are several new stories in the collection. Most of the existing tales will remain unchanged, except for eliminating repetition. The stories in the book can be read on their own, but if read in order, they produce a novel. This was my intent when writing the original stories. When collected in one book, though, I do not need to re-introduce the characters each time, or explain history.

[JE] You first announced this book in the summer of 2005, and publication was slated for late 2006 or early 2007. However, the book did not see the light of day until early 2008. At the Chaosium website, Dustin Wright has mentioned some of the challenges and delays to be found in the publishing world. What were the particular challenges that you faced with this anthology?

[WJ] Publishing has many challenges, but for publishers divided across two industries (games and fiction), the tasks are all the more daunting. Both industries work on different schedules, and reprints are very important in hobby publishing. A role-playing game without its core rulebooks or support books stops selling. This has caused delays in many of Chaosium's fiction books in the past. Likewise, I had hoped to alleviate pressures for Chaosium and myself, by putting off the publishing date. I also needed some extra time for story rights to revert, so although it delayed the book, I think it worked out better in the end.

[JE] There are whispers that Chaosium may be releasing something else from you relatively soon. Is this true?

[WJ] Yes! Chaosium is publishing my book Voodoo Virus. It isn't an anthology or collection; it's a novel. In Chaosium's thirty years of publishing, this will be only their second novel, and the first expansion into a new genre of fiction.

[JE] You've mentioned that there has been growing interest in the film rights to some of your short fiction, specifically "The Tiger" and "The Name of the Enemy." How did you learn about this? Given the choice, which role would you want to play in any film production of your work – consultant and even screenwriter, or distant observer?

[WJ] I was quite surprised by both interests. In my case, I was contacted by a studio producer who had interest in both stories – although he envisioned them with slightly different takes. But given the total number of opportunities in Hollywood, I don't hold high expectations. It is doubtful I'd have any direct influence on the end product. I would be delighted to advise about the characters or stories, but most likely the plots would vary greatly from the originals.

[JE] You teach at a university in Michigan (I don't believe you've ever mentioned the institution's name), and have said in the past that your employer encourages your "extracurricular" activities, especially because they relate to your teachings in literature and film studies. In what other ways does your "day job" intertwine with your fiction writing?

[WJ] I do teach at a university in Michigan, but I tend not to speak of the university because I keep both activities separate – or try. Many of my students know I'm a writer/editor, and others have learned through the university. As I teach English literature, it is easy to blend my careers together. I often write articles on popular fiction topics and deliver them at conferences. I'm presently working on a film studies book that mirrors a class I teach – this helps both in the academic world and in fiction. It also makes it easier for me as a writer, given that publishing is essential to the profession.

[JE] You live in Metamora, Michigan, which seems to be a quaint, historic town. Does the town influence your own dark fiction?

[WJ] I live in a rural area of Metamora – meaning on a dirt road outside of the town. Actually, the road is named "Blood," which is inspiring in itself. Being surrounded by forest and nature, I can often call upon the location for settings or ideas. I'd lived many years in Detroit and other large cities, so I'm quite accustomed to urban life. Moving between the two, at least for me, is very useful. There is a ghost or alien world lurking in every shadow, or creeping along the edge of the woods.

[JE] What is next on the horizon for you? What projects can we expect to see your name on in the coming year?

[WJ] I have a few, although I'm not quite sure of the release schedule. Early in 2008, I believe the Fantasist Enterprises anthology Blood and Devotion will be released, and I have a short story in that titled "The Treachery of Stone." Voodoo Virus should appear around mid-year, and then an anthology I'm editing for Chaosium titled R'lyeh Rising should be published toward the end of 2008. I'm working on a few other projects as well, but I don't have any firm release dates yet.

[JE] It sounds like you have a lot on your plate, as usual. Thanks so much for your time and thoughtful answers, William.

◇◇◇◇◇

Jeff Edwards *is a Staff Reviewer for Dark Wisdom, and is a contributor to The Harrow and SFReader. In the past, he has written reviews for Paradox, Strange Horizons, Lost in the Dark, and Goucher Quarterly. Jeff's fiction has appeared in Potomac Review and Garland.*

Shroud 3 The Journal of Dark Fiction and Art

THE JESUS ORCHID

BY JG FAHERTY

Dr. Richard Penfield leaned back in his leather chair and stared out the window at the Tampa skyline as he contemplated his father's impending death.

The muted buzzing of the intercom interrupted his thoughts, and he turned away from the bright sunshine of a beautiful summer morning. Outside, the temperature was already nearing ninety, but the polarized glass and air conditioning provided an effective barrier against the heat.

"What is it, Jamie?"

"Dr. Boro on line one. She wants to know if you can join her in your father's room."

"Thanks, Jamie. Tell her I'm on my way. Listen, cancel the rest of my appointments, would you? I'll probably be up in Oncology the rest of the afternoon."

"Yes, doctor."

* * *

Damme Boro was waiting for him outside his father's private room. "I'm sorry, Richard."

Penfield hadn't needed to hear any more from the diminutive Nigerian oncologist. How often had he said those same words to a patient, right before delivering news of a terminal illness?

"The cancer has spread too far. There's really nothing more we can do, except make him comfortable and wait." She made an entry on Owen Penfield's chart and then placed a hand on Richard's arm.

"I can have one of our Hospice counselors meet with you later."

"Thanks, Damme, but that won't be necessary." Richard turned away. He felt his friend's concerned gaze on his back, but he needed time alone, to think, before he spoke to anyone.

"I'm going to sit with him a while. I'll call you later."

Behind him, the sound of leather on tile told him Damme was respecting his privacy and leaving him alone.

Alone with the fading husk of his father.

Richard pulled the padded chair up to his father's bed, and tried to ignore the odors of antiseptic, bleach, and urine that drifted through the room. The same smells he never noticed when walking through the halls, or examining his own patients, now seemed sickeningly apparent.

Owen Penfield's room was silent except for the muted beep of the monitor tracking his vitals, and the periodic clicks from the IV unit delivering glucose and morphine into his shrunken arm. The long needle protruded like a torture device from the elder Dr. Penfield's dry, hanging skin.

Hematomas mottled the once-tanned flesh, evidence the staff was finding it increasingly difficult to locate a good vein. Richard Penfield looked away, choosing to stare at his father's face, where signs of the raging cancer were less evident.

In earlier years, people had often commented on how alike the two looked, resembling older and younger brother more than father and son.

Is that how I'm going to look in thirty years? Sagging skin, hair falling out, wasted away to a shell of what I once was?

Richard had no illusions about death; he saw it every day. But that didn't make him less anxious, fearful even, of growing old. If anything, his profession reminded him daily just how short life could be.

A metallic clatter from the doorway startled him, and he turned to see a woman from housecleaning emptying the room's waste can.

"Sorry, doctor suh, I didn't means to startle ya."

The woman, who looked to be a likely client for his cardiovascular surgical team, based on the sixty or seventy extra pounds she carried on her wide frame, gently set the basket back down.

"It's all right. He's my father, not my patient," Penfield said. Her southern accent, with more than a little Creole or Haitian patois thrown in, reminded him of the housekeepers his father had kept, back when everyone had lived at home.

"Dat's yo pappa? Sorry, doctor man. My goodness, he don' look well." The woman came further into the room, stood by the bottom of the bed.

"He's not. He's dying. He has an aggressive lymphoma. Cancer," he added, noticing the look on her face.

"Uh-huh. Da cancer's gon' git you ever' time." She paused, and Richard thought she might leave then, but she didn't.

"Pardon me, but ain't you Doctor Penfield?"

That caught his attention. "Yes, I am. Do we know each other?"

He looked closely at her, thinking maybe she hadn't always worn her hair in cornrows, or been so heavy, but nothing about her dark, island features triggered any recognition. Her pupils had an odd, slightly elliptical shape to them, something he knew he'd have remembered if he'd seen her before.

"No, but I knows 'bout you. Missy Sanchez tol' me how you save her from chokin' in da cafeteria last year. Said you's one a da good ones."

"That's very kind of her. But it wasn't anything special." Just a Heimlich maneuver to dislodge a piece of apple pie crust so large he'd been surprised the woman had fit it into her throat.

"Naw, see, dat's what I mean. Too modest. Missy left Tampa 'fore she could pay you back. Maybe I can do dat for her. My mamma always say return a good deed wit another."

Richard started to say it wasn't necessary, but the woman spoke over his objections.

"Listen heah, doctor man. You take yoself down to Homestead. Go to dis address." She handed Penfield a scrap of paper with an address scrawled on it. "Ask for Gator Daddy. Tell 'im Evalina sent you, dat you need his help."

"Help? Help with what?"

"Wit Mistuh Owen here, dat's what. Now, don' ask me not'ing else. I gots work ta do." She paused at the door, fixed her catlike eyes on him.

"Jus' remembah, you listen to da Daddy. Do what he say, tings be good."

Penfield tried to get her to say more, but she just shook a sausage-shaped finger at him and pushed her cleaning cart out of the room.

What the hell was that about? *And how had she known his father's name?* Richard left his vigil and went into the hall, intending to demand an explanation.

He found himself staring at an empty corridor. Richard asked at the Nurse's Station, but no one had seen the heavy black woman with the Caribbean accent.

Figuring she must have taken the elevator to another floor, Penfield returned to his father's side.

Nothing had changed.

For the next three hours, they stayed like that, father and son, neither one moving.

By the time he went home for dinner, Richard had already forgotten the cleaning woman and her offer.

* * *

Evalina returned to him that night, surrounded by scabrous-looking tendrils from which miniature alligator heads burst forth to snap at him. Her glowing, amber eyes seemed more reptilian than feline.

"Ask for Gator Daddy. Tell 'im Evalina sent you."

Richard sat up in bed, wide awake.

Evalina. Gator Daddy.

Something about making his father all right again. He lay back on his thick pillow.

The dream seemed so real. It...

The sudden ringing of the phone sent his heart into overdrive, to the point where for a moment he feared it might turn arrhythmic.

"Hello?" He waited for the bad

news, the only kind that comes at two in the morning.

Damme's voice. "Richard, your father..."

"I'll be right there."

Forty minutes later, he stood in his father's room again. The elder Penfield's face looked the same, but now the gown had been stripped back, and red marks on the bony chest indicated the shock cart in the corner had already been put to use.

"Richard, there you are." Dr. Boro pulled him away from the bustling nurses who were busy setting up new IVs and injecting medications.

"How is he?"

"Not good. We've stabilized him, but I doubt it will be much longer. Perhaps another day or two."

Ask for Gator Daddy.

Penfield twitched.

"Richard? Are you all right?"

"What? Oh, yes, fine. Listen, I have to go away, it's...an emergency. I'll be back tomorrow. Just keep him alive until then?"

"You're leaving town? Now?"

"Please, Damme, it's important. Do whatever you have to, but don't let him die until I get back."

Boro stared at him for a moment, then nodded. "We'll do what we can. But I can't make any promises, not for someone in his condition."

Richard touched Boro's hand. "Thanks. It means a lot to me."

* * *

I75 South to Naples. Alligator Alley West to Lauderdale. 95 South to Homestead. Penfield re-read the directions he'd hurriedly pulled off MapQuest. Two hundred and thirty miles.

If Damme had known what he'd planned, she'd have probably signed papers indicating he wasn't fit to make medical decisions for his father. Not after leaving him dying in the hospital, to go on some kind of wild goose chase. And for what? Because some cleaning woman said there was a man who could *maybe* help?

But that was the crux of the matter. What if this Gator Daddy *could* help? He was willing to try anything at this point, herbal remedies, holy water, even voodoo spells. Anything to have a few more days, or hours, to say the things he needed to say.

Alligator Alley is a popular tourist road during the day, but at three in the morning, it's more like a time tunnel, a road to the primeval.

Alligators, snakes, and armadillos rule Florida's roads and highways after midnight, creating organic speed bumps for the unwary and uncaring. Red eyes reflect hellishly from canals and sloughs, where descendents of Mesozoic reptiles and protomammals still exist much as their ancestors did.

Driving that seemingly endless eighty-mile stretch, it was too easy to imagine prehistoric creatures, or the ghosts of Seminole Indians, hiding amidst the sawgrass marshes, hammocks, and cypress heads.

Richard kept the window rolled down, letting the moist air, redolent of mud, animal musk, and lush plant life combine with the loud music blasting from his stereo to create a sensory barrage that kept him awake. As a doctor, he was all too aware of how many drivers fell asleep and crashed into the canals each year.

Now the morning sun was hot and bright as it struck the driver's side of his silver-toned BMW 545i, and the exit for Homestead was coming up. He touched the scrap of paper in his pocket.

Thirty minutes later, Richard finished winding his way westward through the side streets of the somnambulant town and pulled up in front of a rundown house whose backyard bordered against the edge of the Everglades.

He knocked on the wooden door, flecks of paint falling away under the attack of his knuckles. After a moment, tired, shuffling footsteps approached, and the door opened to reveal a wiry, dark-skinned man of indeterminate race and age.

Tiny streams of sweat ran down the man's forehead, coming together above his nose to create a large river that flowed down one cheek, mimicking the flow of waters into the Everglades themselves. Yellow stains on his wifebeater t-shirt provided evidence of multiple cycles of perspiration and hasty washing.

"Good morning," Richard said.

The man responded with a cold stare, his blank expression conveying hatred more efficiently than any scowl. Stale, rank sweat, exotic food, and the odor of mildew pushed out from inside the house, an odiferous bodyguard forcing Penfield back a step.

"Perhaps you can help me? I'm looking for someone…"

"No one here." The man started to close the door.

"His name is Gator Daddy," Richard hurriedly added. "Evalina sent me."

The door paused in mid-swing, and the man's belligerent expression gave way to wide eyes. He made a quick sign of the cross, ended it by kissing his thumb.

"You wait here. Pedro help you." The door finished closing.

The rancid aromas of the house's interior lingered heavily in the muggy morning air, and Richard was only too happy to remain on the sagging stoop.

"You da doctor man?"

Richard jumped at the voice behind him, then turned to see who'd spoken.

A young boy, maybe ten or twelve years old, stood at the bottom of the stairs. His brown skin, straight black hair, and thin facial features gave him away as one of the local Spanish-Indian mix breeds, descendants of the original Indians who'd inhabited the swamps when the conquistadors first arrived.

The boy moved closer, looking Richard up and down with eyes so dark they seemed black, except for a tiny ring of greenish-gold around the pupils. If anything, he was even dirtier than the man who'd answered the door. But where that man had worn his anger like clothing, the boy exuded an almost mischievous happiness.

Richard nodded.

"I'm Pedro. I take you to da Daddy. Out in da swamps. Daddy got da cure you need. Cost you fifty dollars." The boy held out his hand and smiled, showing teeth stained brown from years of neglect.

"How do you know what I need?" Richard asked.

"Evalina tol' me you be coming. But we got to go now. Ain't good to be out in da swamp after dark."

* * *

Behind the house, past a small back yard littered with car parts, festering piles of fish guts, and something that looked like a dead armadillo hanging from a frayed clothesline, sat a beat-up, rusted airboat. The yard itself was more prehistoric coral reef than grass, and it dipped down to the edge of the water. Less than two feet further, the tall saw grass began its reign.

"I drive," Pedro said, displaying one of his decay-filled smiles.

Richard looked towards the house, not happy about leaving civilization and going out into the swamp.

"Don' worry, your car safe. Nobody mess wit' Gator Daddy's kin." Pedro started the engine, which caught with a gigantic roar, sending nearby waterfowl into the air. Clouds of oily, black smoke belched out as the great fan propelled them away from shore.

Although he'd lived in Florida all his life, it was Penfield's first ride in an airboat. He held on with a white-knuckled grip as Pedro flew the howling machine across the water, destroying the pristine silence and leaving startled animals and birds in their wake.

They snaked their way around pine hammocks and cypress stands, cut through fields of overgrown lily pads, crossed large expanses of open water, and ploughed through forests of saw grass prairies.

Richard made an attempt to remember landmarks in case he needed to find his way back alone, but gave up after only a few minutes. His minimal knowledge of the Everglades ecosystem came from what he'd read in the papers, or learned in school as a child. As the minutes stretched into miles, he knew he'd be hopelessly lost without his guide.

They'd left Pedro's derelict home at close to ten a.m.; it was almost twelve-thirty when the boy banked the airboat into a steep turn and brought them to a stop next to a large pine hammock. A small path led from the water up into the trees. Pedro ran the boat partway ashore and cut the engine.

In the stillness that followed, white noise buzzed in Richard's head as his ear drums gradually recovered from their beating. Slowly the sounds of the swamp returned in cheeps, trills, and grunts.

"Now we wait." Pedro reached under his seat, pulled out a ratty, oil-stained baseball cap, the team emblem long since worn away. He pulled the hat low over his eyes and put his head down.

"Wait? Wait for what?"

"This heah's Gator Daddy's island. I don' know where he be just now. Could be close, could be far. But he hear da boat. He comin'."

For the next fifteen minutes, Richard sat and stared at the murky waters, a whirlwind of conflicting thoughts spinning around his head. He should be with his father, not in some godforsaken swamp. Why was he even here?

Finally, he couldn't take it anymore and decided to explore the trail, just to take his mind off everything. The island was only about a hundred yards in length; there was no way he could get lost. He stepped out of the boat carefully, cringing when his Topsiders sank into the soft soil that at its highest point rose only two or three feet above the water line.

The skinny slash pines offered meager shade from the afternoon sun, and Richard felt the first tingling of sunburn beneath his thinning hair.

Bright green air plants nestled in the crooks of tree limbs and clung to trunks, identical to the ones Richard saw every day attached to the palm trees in his yard. Only here the thick, bristling leaves seemed much larger. Many sprouted bright red and orange flowers, which he'd never seen the ones at home do.

He waved at the clouds of mosquitoes that had descended on him as soon as he left the boat. For each one he killed, it seemed as if twenty took its place. He cursed out loud, then stopped when several of the miniature vampires flew into his mouth.

Pedro glanced over and laughed. "Hoo, man, little flies like your blood, doctor man. Maybe dey suck you dry 'fore you leave."

"Hopefully we won't be here that long." Richard tried to wipe the bugs from his tongue, but only made things worse as he smeared the ones on his hand across his lips. "I'm going to see if this Alligator Daddy is here. Maybe he didn't hear us."

"Mistah doctor man, you go in dere, maybe you not come out. Snakes, spiders, 'gators, dey like da hammocks. Good place to sleep, good place to hunt. Out heah you jus' dinner."

Richard looked at the slash pines standing to either side of the path. A gentle splash sounded as a blue heron scooped a fish from the water near the boat and took off again. Farther into the swamp something bellowed, a primitive noise.

A mosquito landed on Richard's left eye, got caught in the lashes.

"Fine, I'll wait in the boat." At least the mosquitoes weren't bothering him there.

Now, I wonder why that is?

Another bellow in the distance. This one was answered by a heart-rending wail that reminded Penfield of the time a woman came into the emergency room having lost both her legs in a car accident.

"What the hell was that?"

"Sound like a big cat, what dey call panther. I tink Daddy prob'ly on his way."

"How do you know?"

Pedro didn't answer, but Richard thought he caught a hint of a smile.

Silence re-asserted itself. The occasional splash of something entering or leaving the water would draw Richard's head one way or the other, but always too late to see the culprit.

Two turtles sat motionless on a tree stump ten feet from shore.

Overhead, turkey vultures sailed on the thermals, spiraling up until they were mere dots against the blue.

A ripple in the water, but nothing broke the surface.

"He's heah."

Pedro's voice was quiet, but before Richard could ask where, a deep, gravelly voice spoke from behind him.

"Whatchoo need?"

"Shit!" Richard stumbled back, and only a desperate grab for his seat kept him from falling overboard.

Gliding up next to the airboat was a small, wooden dinghy. A tall, heavyset figure stood in the center, using a long pole to propel the boat along.

Gator Daddy stood well over

six feet, a fact even his stooped posture couldn't hide. He wore faded green cut-off shorts, and a t-shirt so stained and covered in swamp muck it was impossible to tell if it had started life white or yellow. A dead Florida panther occupied the back portion of the boat. Blood still dripped from the hole in its neck.

Richard glanced into the boat, but couldn't see a gun.

The man's grizzled beard made a half-hearted attempt to hide his distinctly unusual bone structure. Random bulges pushed outward along the jaw line, and similar protuberances marred his forehead.

"Doctor man, this heah Gator Daddy," Pedro said with a knowing smile that was older than his years.

An odor assaulted Richard, a disagreeable smell that somehow seemed part of the Everglades, yet different. Mud, swamp, musk; it was all of those, but none of them. Underneath it lurked something less natural, something reminiscent of the sick breath of his dying patients.

Pedro clapped his hands and laughed. "Doctor man a-scared of Gator Daddy!"

An owl, startled from its roost, glided low over their heads and then back up to a tree further away.

"Speak up, man. I got betta t'ings ta do den stan' heah jawin' wit da likes o' you." The bass tones of Gator Daddy's voice vibrated skin and bones.

Richard ignored the rapid pounding in his chest and found his voice. "Evalina said you could help my father." The words cracked coming out, and he cleared his throat.

Gator Daddy spat a mouthful of reddish-brown liquid on the thin soil, exposing rows of overly-large, stained, pointed teeth in the process. Something that looked like wet fur was wedged between two of them.

"Aye-huh. He dyin', yo' pappa?"

"Yes." The word came out hard; even now, with only hours to go, he could barely admit it.

Gator Daddy poled the boat to the edge of the hammock, got out and pulled it up out of the water. Muscles bulged in his forearms and under his shirt.

"Dis way." He headed up the path.

Pedro jumped out and followed, leaving Richard to climb out, leather shoes slipping and sliding in the wet marl. He hurried to catch up, keeping a watchful eye for snakes and spiders at the same time.

The Haunted Wood

Tools and Toys

for the MAGICALLY MINDED

Handmade altars, wands, staves, staffs, athames, chalices, besoms, runes, ogham, boxes and more.

Rare and Unique Woods including:

Almond wood, Holly, English Yew, and Irish Bog Oak, and much more.

New England's preminent Pagan/Wiccan resource.

visit us today at:

www.hauntedwoodcrafts.com

...

graphix studio
logo design • screen printed clothing
design & sales   drew davis
603 • 969 • 4987   anamgraphix@aol.com

After only a few yards the path split, one branch heading deeper into the trees, the other curving back to the water. It was down this second branch that Gator Daddy led them. He stopped at the island's edge, where a tall, heavy tree raised gnarled root stumps from the water.

"Dis heah a pond cypress. Whatchoo see dere, doctor man?"

Richard shook his head. A few ubiquitous air plants clung to the ridged, grayish-green trunk, and Spanish moss hung in spider-web fashion from the lower branches.

"What am I supposed to see?"

"Da cure." A thick, yellow-green fingernail tapped a tiny bulge on the trunk.

Richard peered closer. What he'd at first thought was a ridge of bark was in actuality a small web of roots, exactly the same color as the tree they clung to. Once he could see it, he realized others occupied places on the tree as well.

"Is that another plant, like these?" Richard pointed to one of the common, bright green varieties attached nearby.

"It be a plant, but not like none other. Dis one is da Jesus Orchid."

"Jesus Orchid? You mean it's a flower?" Penfield turned away. He felt like an ass, coming halfway across the state for nothing.

"Not jus' a flower, doctor man. Dis flower give life by eatin' death."

Richard stopped walking, looked back.

"Yeah, dat right, doctor man. Life. When yo' medicines no good, da Jesus Orchid work jus' fine. Da Spanish, dey called dis place El Laguno del Espirito Sanctu. Lake of de Holy Spirit. Da Jesus Orchid jus' one miracle hidin' in dese swamps."

Gator Daddy patted a hand against the tree. "Dis cypress already heah when my daddy found out 'bout da Jesus Orchid from a Calusa medicine man."

"Calusa? You mean Seminole. The Spaniards wiped out the Calusas in the seventeen hundreds."

"You listen, doctor man." Foul-smelling spittle sprayed out from Gator Daddy's mouth, and his voice grew louder. "I said Calusa. My daddy, he named Alvarez. He sailed heah wit Cap'n de Aviles in fi'teen sixty-five. Married hisself a Calusa woman ten years later."

"So I'm supposed to believe you're how old? A hundred years? Because of some plant?"

"More'n two hunnert." Gator Daddy raised his t-shirt. Flakes of dried mud crumbled off in the process.

Richard stepped back a pace from the bitter tang of the man's odor.

A fine pattern of scales covered Gator Daddy's belly and chest from waist to nipples. In the dappled sunlight, they shone with a greenish, mother-of-pearl patina.

Sitting where his navel should have been was a Jesus Orchid, the filamentous roots woven around the scales and penetrating the skin between. In the center of the plant, a small red flower bud, hardly larger than a pencil eraser, stood out in stark detail against the camouflaging pale green of the parasitic plant.

"My daddy stuck dis on me when I been forty-eight, and dyin' o' da measles. Cured me up da next day, an' I ain't never been sick since, never grown no older."

Against his will, against all scientific sensibilities, hope sprouted in Richard's heart.

"But...the scales. Did it do that to you?"

Gator Daddy drew his shirt down. "No, I born wit dose. Daddy's wife also da medicine man's daughter. 'Cordin' to him, she weren't quite human. Guess dis heah boy take after his mamma."

Richard tried to comprehend what he'd seen and heard, and found it was too much for him. Instead, he changed the subject.

"So how do I use the Jesus Orchid to save my father?"

"Simple, doctor man. You takes one back wit you, put it on yo daddy. Best place be da chest or belly, no one else see it dat way. You wait. Next mornin', he be on his feet again."

He drew a small folding knife from one pocket. "You got a bag, son?"

Richard started to shake is head, thinking the question was for him, but Pedro answered.

"Yeah, I brought it." The young boy handed over a plastic bag, the kind you'd put a sandwich in.

Gator Daddy pried one of the Jesus Orchids off the tree, holding the bag so the plant fell into it. Then he sealed the zip lock top and handed it to Richard.

"Now, you listen, doctor man. Two tings you got to know. Don' touch it, no matter what. You touch it, it become part of you, never come off. Jus' open da bag and shake it out onto yo' daddy. It do da rest itself."

"That's it?" Richard took the bag. The Jesus Orchid felt warm, even through the plastic. He slipped it into his pocket.

"No. Other ting is, if yo daddy dead 'fore you can use it, that's it. Not'ing bring back da dead. You can burn it, you can keep it fo' yo'self. But don' put it on da dead."

"What would happen?"

Gator Daddy looked at him with green eyes flecked in gold, and for the first time Richard realized the man's pupils were elliptical slits, like Evalina's.

Like an alligator's.

"Not'ing good, doctor man. Not'ing good."

* * *

"Code Blue, Room 713. Code Blue, Room 713." The elevator doors opened to the sound of the matter-of-fact announcement.

Oh, no. Dad.

Richard ran down the hallway, joining the nurses heading for his father's room. Dr. Boro was already inside, calling for epinephrine and signaling for someone to charge the crash cart.

"Damme, do something!"

"I'm trying, Richard, but his body is too weak."

A nurse pulled Richard away. "Please, Doctor Penfield, give them room."

Richard wrung his hands as his father's body spasmed under the paddles. In his pocket, the Jesus orchid grew warmer, as if sensing the presence of someone in need of its curative powers.

After the third attempt, Dr. Boro hung up the defibrillator paddles. "Stop compressions. Time of death, four twenty-three a.m." She turned to Richard. "I'm sorry, Richard. I..."

"No! Move out of the way!" Richard pushed a nurse aside and ran to his father, fumbling to pull the Jesus Orchid from his pocket.

"Don' put it on da dead."

The warning popped into his head as he opened the plastic bag.

But he's not dead! His heart was beating just a moment ago.

"You listen to da Daddy. Do what he say, tings be good."

Now Evalina's voice had joined in, but it was too late.

The Jesus orchid dropped out of the bag onto his father's chest. The moment the dry, stiff roots touched flesh, the plant came to life, extending filamentous tendrils in every direction, which quickly penetrated the skin. The color of the plant changed from dull gray to pale tan, nearly disappearing against the skin of its new host.

In the center of the plant, a tiny, red flower blossomed.

"Jesus, Richard! What the hell did you do?"

Dr. Boro stepped forward, but Richard held her back with one arm.

"No, Damme. Leave it alone. It's a cure. Just watch, and then I'll explain everything."

The oncologist started to say something, but just then the body on the bed opened its eyes, tried to speak around the tube in its throat.

"Good god, what's happening?" Boro asked in a low voice.

"Not'ing good, doctor man. Not'ing good."

Richard heard the rumbling voice, and this time it was accompanied by the musky odor of the swamp, and a vision of the man shaking his head. Next to him, Pedro laughed, his rotten teeth like ancient corn in his small mouth.

Richard's father sat up, pulled the tube from his throat. "Richard," he croaked.

"See? He's alive!"

"No, Richard." Damme pointed at the monitor, where all the vital signs showed as straight lines. "What have you done?"

Richard ignored her, moved closer as his father raised a hand towards him.

* * *

At the seventh floor nurses' station, Debbie Ramirez spilled her coffee when the first screams started in Room 713.

* * *

Deep in the Pa-hay-okee, west of Homestead, small epiphytes growing on a lone cypress began to pulse and change color from grayish-brown to deep red.

A young boy laughed.

⸺⸺

JG Faherty's work has appeared in several magazines, e-zines, and anthologies; most recently his story "Bones" was accepted for Cemetery Dance issue #58 (winter 2007). He also had "Family First" accepted for this year's Garden State Horror Writers Dark Territories anthology. In addition, he'll have a story in MagusZine this winter.

Visit our forums and our blog by clicking on our Web site

www.shroudmagazine.com

WWW.BRIANKEENE.COM
$7.99 EACH
NEW HORROR!

SHROUD PUBLISHING
IS A
PROUD MEMBER
OF THE HORROR WRITERS' ASSOCIATION
AND THE NEW ENGLAND HORROR WRITERS

PLEASE SUPPORT OUR AUTHORS AND ARTISTS

WWW.SHROUDMAGAZINE.COM

THANK YOU!

Shroud 3 The Journal of Dark Fiction and Art

GRIMOIRES AND TOMES

Book Reviews

HEBREW PUNK, Lavie Tidhar
Review by I.E. Lester

Lavie Tidhar's prose is raw, occasionally even harsh. He doesn't produce the polished prose of Ray Bradbury or the fully developed characters of Stephen King, but despite the use of several typical, and much over-used, staples of horror - zombies, vampires, werewolves and the like - his fiction is fresh.

Each of these monsters enters against a background of Jewish mythology; Tidhar's vampires don't fear crosses; his zombies are golems - animated beings created from inanimate matter, raised and controlled by a dark Rabbi; his fallen angel is a former immortal Tzaddik ("Righteous One"). From a non-European tradition, Tidhar's monsters are reborn, given new afterlife.

He also doses his stories with a great deal of humour, and a wonderfully bizarre look at the world. The opening tale, "The Heist," introduces Tidhar's characters wonderfully well, bringing them together in an attempted raid on the city's magick-filled, Fort Knox-like, blood bank.

"Transylvania Mission" moves the action to World War II, pitting the Jewish undead against Nazi werewolf commandos in Castle Dracula.

Tidhar relocates the conflict further back in time in "Uganda," in which the Rabbi (the golem controller from "The Heist") accompanys a scouting party in Africa that is hoping to establish a Jewish homeland. As well as roughly sharing the same time-period as Bram Stoker's Dracula, the story also shares the novel's structure as Tidhar relates the tale through diary entries, letters and various documents.

The fourth yarn follows the Tzaddik, now a drug addict, to the seedier side of 1920s London. Throw in ghosts, gangsters, and eastern assassins, and you have a great story - the strongest of the four, and by far, the darkest.

Hebrew Punk is a short set, lasting a mere one hundred and forty-seven large print pages, and as such, it only allows a taste of the author's potential. However, Hebrew Punk is highly entertaining stuff. In addition, considering its inclusion of a great amount of Hebrew law and tradition, Tidhar's writing impresses in the fact that the reader requires no prior knowledge of the Jewish faith to enjoy the stories.

He's not the finished article by any means, but this reviewer believes Lavie Tidhar has quite the future ahead of him.

Available on Amazon.com for $11.86

POE, A LIFE CUT SHORT, Peter Ackroyd
Review by I.E. Lester

One of the fathers of crime and horror fictions, Edgar Allan Poe's tales and poems include the absolute

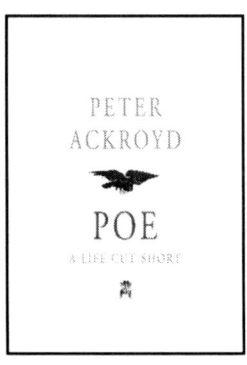

classics "The Murders in the Rue Morgue", "The Fall of the House of Usher" and "The Raven." So the chance to find out about the man himself is definitely worth taking.

Well you may find yourself wishing you hadn't. Poe's character is not a pleasant one - he's not a person you would want as a friend - and biographer Peter Ackroyd certainly doesn't hide some of the less reputable parts of Poe's character and life. If he had, Poe: a Life Cut Short would have been, well, cut short.. Perhaps he should have.

However, despite his not hiding Poe's faults, you do get the feeling that Ackroyd almost apologises for his subject. He describes Poe as prone to drinking heavily and showing a dependency on alcohol, but denies that the man was an alcoholic. It feels like the biographer splits hairs somewhat.

Ackroyd has attempted to show how Poe's situation, both geographic and historic, influences his life, his character, and his fiction. He describes the relatively poor social status and early death of Poe's parents, the lack of affection or approval from his foster father, and the ill health and premature death of his wife, and how these affects Poe and his state of mind.

Many of Ackroyd's conclusions make sense, although at times his attempts to explain why Poe was the man he was serve only to show him as a whining paranoid. Poe was a brilliant author (that's beyond doubt), but as a man, he was less than admirable.

The most apparent thing about the book itself is the level of research. Ackroyd has done his homework. The problem is that he shows this off to too great an extent, resulting in a book that is more scholarly than an average horror fan might want.

This is biography where fact follows fact, rather than a narrative - an academic work not a story - with Poe's life presented largely in the form of extracts from letters interspersed with details of his writing and editing life. Thankfully, it cuts itself short.

One hundred sixty pages makes this a very survivable book, where three hundred pages of fact following fact may have been beyond the capabilities of even the most determined reader and Poe fan. Poe: a Life Cut Short is a very informative book, and there's a good deal to recommend it. Just don't expect an exciting read.

$14.93; Hardcover; Amazon.com

AGNES HAHN, Richard Satterlie
Review by I.E. Lester

Agnes Hahn is the archetypal wallflower. She dresses plainly, avoiding any suggestion of femininity, in oversized flannel shirts and works at an animal sanctuary. Her life can be categorised with one word - dull. So when she is arrested, suspected of being a sexually-themed serial killer (the wonderfully nicknamed "Menstrual Killer," due to the type of evidence left at the crime scenes) it really does get a reader's attention.

Reporter Jason Powers accepts the assignment to investigate the case. The only problem is that he has a history with Art Bransome, the detective in charge of the investigation. Their last encounter saw Powers expose a forensics lab whose faulty evidence had convicted an innocent man. Not a problem in itself, except that his work had also caused other, obviously guilty, parties to be released, resulting in further attacks and murders.

To further his antagonism of Bransome, Powers is convinced that Agnes is innocent and uncovers evidence that casts doubt on the seemingly incontrovertible DNA results - Agnes has an identical twin (unknown even to her), and Powers believes that sister Lilin is the real killer.

Not much in this novel is new. The long-lost twin trope is not new; doubt cast on a suspect despite a great deal of compelling evidence has appeared before. Having Powers and Bransome work together to solve the case, concurrently resolving their differences is also a familiar plot device. In addition, even the twists in the plot read like deja vu.

However, the author has skillfully imbued the story with suspense - impressive when one considers the predictable aspects of the story. His characters live. His locations – spring three-dimensionally from each page.

Satterlie accomplishes this by using our knowledge of the form. He uses partial stereotypes, adding subtle differences to the standard players expected in these tales, confounding expectations enough to make them interesting.

Satterlie has produced the kind of book Stephen King might have written twenty years ago, although admittedly (or thankfully) not as verbose as King. Agnes Hahn grips the reader, and be warned that it may cause you to lose sleep.

However, this isn't because it's scary. Even when one considers the horror is very real and not supernatural, there are instances that are perturbing to say the least (especially for male readers). It's one of those books that you will decide on just one more chapter before you turn out the light (for the eighth time that night).

$7.99; MM PB; Amazon.com

∞∞∞∞∞∞∞∞∞∞∞∞∞∞∞∞∞∞∞∞

OLD FLAMES, Jack Ketchum
Review by I.E. Lester

Jack Ketchum continues his mastery in presenting characters that are terrifically nuanced and sympathetic yet unbalanced, creating in the reader a mixed bag of emotion.

In Leisure's Old Flames, Dora Welles is a fortyish woman living in New York. Her latest relationship has just gone the way of all the others. She encounters an old school friend in a bar who tells her of "Flame Finders," a private detective service that will track down anyone from your past. Dora asks them to find Jim Weybourne, her high school sweetheart.

Jim, she discovers, has everything that she wants, the happy family, the stable life, everything. Despite this, she decides to meet up with him - inventing a business trip and arranging an "accidental" encounter in a bar near Jim's Californian home. Dora infiltrates Jim's life with ease, although not for the friendly purposes Jim imagines.

It's not exactly original; this kind of story has been done many times before. Fortunately, though, the story is short, spanning only 130 pages. Not too long for the familiarity to grate on the nerves (rather than fray them), but long enough to develop his lead character fully. {Tim, I do not know what the previous sentence means}

Dora is unbalanced, seriously unhinged. A succession of failed relationships have left her near broken, and she has latched onto a thread, one that might bring some lasting happiness to her life, and she is determined to have it - never mind the consequences to anyone else.

Dora is the absolute star of Ketchum's novel - pretty much everything and everyone else is incidental to a story of a person going seriously off the rails.

–Also included in the book is a "bonus" (and slightly longer) novella called "Right to Life." Sara Foster is accidentally pregnant. As the father is married (and not likely to change that), she chooses to have a termination.

Things don't go to plan though. Sara is drugged and abducted outside the entrance of the abortion clinic, and awakens far from New York, imprisoned in a long narrow box in the basement of a small, isolated house.

Her captors subject her to a serious of humiliations and tortures designed to break her spirit. They keep her naked, tied, and gagged, beating and whipping her often, taunting her with accurate details of her friends and family, and what they will do to them if she refuses to submit..

Brutality if "Right to Life"'s mantra.. However, demeaning "Right to Life" is to Sara for much of its length, she is portrayed as a strong woman, one determined not to give in or lose herself. There is always the feeling in the story that her time will come, that she will get a chance to strike back.

> Shroud is interested in reviewing published works of dark speculative fiction.
>
> Please send advance review copies at least one month before publication date, accompanied by appropriate press materials. Shroud is also available for jacket blurbs provided that the content is sent well-enough in advance.
>
> Other books can be sent at any time with the understanding that we cannot guarantee that we will review everything and review materials cannot be returned. Sorry!
>
> Send review materials (books, DVDs, Games, CDs) to:
>
> Shroud Publishing
> 121 Mason Rd.
> Milton, NH 03851
>
> Questions? editor@shroudmagazine.com

As with "Old Flames,", there is a familiar tone to "Right to Life." - a tone not unique within Ketchum's own backlist. The Girl Next Door has a similar torture theme, while novels like Joyride, The Lost, and Off Season also contain themes of torment and human distress which often culminate in redemption via severe injury and even death to major characters

The violence verges on excessive at times. The glee and arousal displayed by Sara's captor during her torture is pornographic and, at times, difficult to read. Violence perpetrated by otherworldly or demonic beings is relatively easy on the stomach. Monsters from other planets and from the bowels of the earth do not exist. However, human monsters do exist and Ketchum's violence is violence presented as mundane, often merely plot device; one human being deliberately inflicting pain on an unwilling victim for pleasure. The reader becomes desensitized after a while and numbly reads, travelling from one sadistic act to the next without real inflection.

However, Old Flames is very well written. But be warned: you are not in for an easy ride here.

Leisure Horror MM PB $7.99

SAINT-GERMAIN: MEMOIRS, By Chelsea Quinn Yarbro

Review by Chris Welch

Some vampires age better than others. Some have a certain class, a certain virtuosity, a certain aristocratic demeanor connoted by their very name. Dracula, Lestat, and Barnabas Collins, for example, sit at the head of the table of sophisticated vampire mythology.

Of course, there is a fourth chair at the table belonging to Chelsea Quinn Yarbro's Saint-Germain, a long-popular character — first appearing in Hotel Transylvania in 1971, and then being the focus of four more novels; The Palace, Blood Games, Path of Eclipse, and Tempting Fate. There is also a collection of stories, Saint-Germain: Chronicles, which contains stories written in the 1970s and 1980s.

A new Saint-Germain collection, Saint-Germain: Memoirs from Elder Signs Press, collects five modern shorter works of Yarbro's gentleman vampire, two short stories, two novelettes, and a novella. Three are reprints from other anthologies, but the 10,000 word "Lost Epiphany" and the 42,000 word "Tales Out of School" are unique to this collection.

If you are familiar with Saint-Germain, this collection will be like a visit from an old friend.

If you have never read a Saint-Germain novel before, this collection will be a nice introduction to the character. If unfamiliar with his creator, you must make that acquaintance right away, as Yarbro's literary finesse is the only thing more impressive than her historical verisimilitude.

She writes with an artist's eye for detail, a linguist's love for language, and a scholar's accuracy for truth.

The collection begins with "Harpy," in which Saint-Germain meets the neglected family of a rebellious philosopher in ancient Greece. "Lost Epiphany" concerns early Christian-era monks and pirates, and Saint-Germain has to discern who the real sinner in the conflict is. "A Gentleman of the Old School" brings Saint-Germain into the 21st Century, as he helps an investigative reporter stop a serial killer in modern-day Vancouver, Canada.

The two stand-out tales in this collection are "Intercession" and "Tales Out of School."

"Intercession" is an epistolary story set in the Spanish colonies of the mid-1600s New World. Penned by Rogerio, Saint-Germain's loyal servant, the letters detail Rogerio's investigation as to why the Inquisition has taken Saint-Germain prisoner, and why they keep moving him from prison to prison across South America.

"A Gentleman of the Old School" occurs at the onset of the Italian Renaissance in the early 1300s. Two interweaving plots involve Saint-Germain's newly acquired position at a University teaching young and somewhat troublesome students how to mix herbs for medicine, and a young widow named Orazia. She suffers from some fatal ailment, and Saint-Germain offers her a cure — becoming a vampire like himself. However, can Orazia make a decision that she feels is against her Church teachings? And will her brother-in-law, a power hungry priest, interfere in the decision?

A bonus aspect to Saint-Germain: Memoirs is Yarbro's afterword, in which she provides insight into the writing process and the character of Saint-Germain. Also, Sharon Russell provides an endearing introduction to the collection as well.

Elder Signs Press/Trade Paperback $14.95

SCORNED
by Joseph McGee

"Just remember me. Is that so much to ask?"
"Yes."
"Why?"
"You're dead!"

He woke up in a cold sweat, startled by the fire that surrounded his bed.

The smoke circled Michael Archer with an acrid stench that curled in his lungs. He gagged on the smoke, turning away from the burning carpet and drapes by the sole window in his bedroom. The smoke closed him in, letting him know that a horrible death was imminent.

The fire alarm took off, beeping a loud, piercing warning to other tenants on the fourth floor of the building complex.

Fire truck sirens blared in the distance.

The window imploded. Archer covered his face with his right arm, shielding his eyes from the glass, but still a few sharp shards pierced his forearm and hand.

The sheets of the bed blazed, blue and yellow dancing flames turning to orange, waving back and forth.

Archer stood on the bed, hugged the wall a few feet from the fire, the burning mouth of the roaring beast closing in on him.

He prayed silently, and before the flame gained another foot, Michael Archer jumped from the foot of the bed, landing on the other side of the fire. He tumbled and rolled in the cloud of grey smoke.

She caught his eye again. This time, she was in the fire, and this was no dream.

The fire seemed to shift toward him now, like it had a mind of its own. The carpet had not been touched this far out, only the foot or so that surrounded the bed was engulfed. There were no scorch marks anywhere else. The wallpaper's colors had not even faded from the enormous heat of the flame. She was in control of it. He wasn't sure how, but he knew it.

He ran to the door, threw it open, escaped down the hall toward the other tenants, who seemed to be evacuating. They all ran down a set of stairs in an aged, narrow hallway. The railing was chipped and dinged, weakened with age, and the walls had been only partially painted, the paint lumpy, greasy, as though a body was stuck behind the walls.

The sirens were closer now, probably just outside. A few moments later, a team of four firefighters rushed in, hurrying the tenants along as they set up a high-pressured house and fitted themselves with oxygen tanks and masks.

Michael Archer, approximately thirty-five years old, a freelance journalist, ran to one of the firefighters. He couldn't see a face through the mask. He could only see a hazy representation of a man in a heavy yellow/black down coat. "My apartment!" Archer told the man. "D3."

The man removed his mask for a moment, and yelled loudly and clearly over the radio. "Fire in D3. Repeat: D3." He rushed up the stairs to the fourth floor of the house, followed by a team of two and then one more with a large heavy-duty fire extinguisher.

One hour later, the fire waned and was co ntained to the one apartment on the fourth floor.

Archer sat on the bumper of an ambulance, paramedics examining him for burns and smoke inhalation. He seemed to have a non-deadly amount of smoke in his system that would clear up relatively soon with the help of rest, water, and the oxygen mask wrapped around his face. One of the paramedics had requested he go to the hospital for further evaluation. Michael agreed to go, but later. His place was in flames, and a girl that appeared in his dreams had shown herself in the fire, guiding it to murder him. Though he knew it was nothing more than his imagination or some vivid hallucination from the underlying circumstances of near death and lack of sleep that past week, he wanted to stick around and see if someone could tell him the fire's cause.

He didn't smoke. The stove wasn't on. He couldn't understand what could have caused it.

A man came over to him in a dark blue suit and tie.

"Are you the resident from D3?"

Michael nodded.

The man in the suit looked at the paramedics. "Is he okay to talk?"

"He's fine," the paramedic answered," but he should be further evaluated at the ER."

"Okay then. I'll ride along."

Michael removed the mask. "Who are you?"

"Detective Dean Gamble. I know this is a bad time, but I have some questions."

Michael knew someone would come and ask questions, but he couldn't help thinking that the detective's response was cliché, as if he watched too many reruns of Law and Order. He was even getting out a pen and a small pad from his inside jacket pocket.

"Do you remember what happened?"

"No." He took a deep breath from the mask and removed it from his face. "I was asleep until I woke up," he coughed. "I just ran for the door."

"It's a miracle you made it out," Gamble said. "The way the bed was in the fire—it's a damn miracle."

Michael took another long drag from the mask, and it helped him fight the urge to cough a bit. Moments later, however, he hacked for a few seconds, panicking briefly when he could'ny catch his breath. He looked around the back of the ambulance. He had never been in one before. He saw the white cabinets with filled medical supplies, locked shelves of medicine and pain relievers, needles, gauze, medical tape, bandages of all kinds and tubes of different shapes and sizes.

"I don't know what started it," he said, the mask muffling his voice. "I just don't know."

"Do you know of anyone who would want to hurt you?"

"No."

"An angry spouse, relative, neighbor, business associate?"

"No. No one," he said. Michael closed his eyes, thinking, seeking a reason why anyone would want to --"Heeeerr," Michael said. "H-h-her!"

And the world spiraled away.

* * *

His eyes blinked open, slowly at first, then his vision pooled together.

Michael lay in a bed in the ER.

A doctor had come in to check in on him. "How are you doing, Mr. Archer?"

His mouth was too cotton-dry to say much of anything.

"Water."

"It's right there for you," the doctor in his blue scrubs said as he pointed to the bed tray. "We checked you out, Mr. Archer, and aside from a few minor scrapes and some smoke in your lungs, you seem to be doing fine."

His lungs were on fire, a burning heat within the flesh, scorching them into ashes.

"I'm Doctor Hines. We're going to keep you for a night and see how you're doing. You lost consciousness for almost an hour, and we're running blood work to make sure everything else is okay."

Michael nodded his head as he sipped through a straw. The cold chill of the ice water bothered his throat, reminding him of when he was seven and has his tonsils removed. It was at the same hospital, too—St. Joseph's

Medical Center.

The room was small. No bigger than a jail cell. The walls were white and lined with white cabinets, white machines, and even white plastic chairs, like the hospital was on some sort of cleanliness strike and needed everything to be the purest color.

They took him by wheelchair from the ER to the second floor for observation. That's where the over-nighters go, with double the nursing staff than on other floors. ICU was on the building's east side, and opposite was Michael and a dozen other patients who had opted to stay for observation.

Michael was lucky to have gotten out of the fire alive, and he knew it.

Someone in the ER had stripped him to his boxers. Heart-monitor tags dotted his chest and an IV slowly dripped into a needle piercing his hand. He wore a light blue and white paper-like hospital gown, like a dental bib from the dentist's office.

Michael was surprised that Doctor Hines didn't offer to call anyone for him. There was no one to call, but the offer would have been appreciated, anyway.

He lay alone, knowing that about every four hours for the next day, someone would come in and check his vitals, draw blood, and ask him how he was feeling, the notorious question one faces on the second floor of the hospital.

The window near his near his bed faced the busy streets catering to traffic and small business. The sun was setting in the autumn sky, leaves blowing off the trees, rushing as if they had something important to do. Michael stared at the caramel sky and wondered what really had happened in his apartment. Who did he see?

He was having a conversation with her like he had known her, and perhaps he did, in some past life. She was sweet, funny, and beautiful in her lacy dress, yet he did not know her name. He thought it may be Isabel, but why would he think that, There'd been no slight mention in his dreams, nor was it a name thst he was ever familiar with. Until this moment. The name had simply dropped into his mind like a coin in a slot.

He didn't want to fall asleep. Michael knew she'd be there waiting for him. But he couldn't just stay up all night, especially not with the sleeping pills they'd given him; they seemed pointless if he was going to be disturbed a few times while trying to fall asleep. Nonetheless, he tried.

The clock above a whiteboard emblazoned with his nurse's name and the current date read 6:28 pm.

He shifted to his side on the painfully thin mattress and drifted off…

Into her world.

* * *

He was in the same hospital room. The only thing that was different was that she—Isabel— was sitting in the blue chair against the blue wall, smiling at him. Her curly blonde hair seemed innocent and sweet, as did her blue eyes. She stood. She was five-foot-seven and couldn't have been more than one hundred and twenty pounds.

"Who are you?"

"You know my name, Michael."

"No, I don't."

"You just don't remember me." Her voice was hollow.

"Why did you try to kill me?"

She tilted her head, confused. "I did not try to kill you, my sweet Michael. I tried to set you free so you could be with me again."

"Be with you again?"

"Why won't you remember?" she said.. "Down by the lake, at your grandparents' house, we first kissed. Two summers after that, we made love on such a cold summer's night—why won't you remember me?"

She walked over to his bedside, hands shaking, eyes bulging out, face blazing with anger and despair. "Why won't you remember me? Why? Why?" She said it over and over until it rang in his head like a mantra. He tried to close his eyes to her anger, his ears to her pleas….

"Knock, knock," the nurse said as she entered carrying a white basket of medical supplies. "Hi, Mr. Archer."

He jerked into a sitting position on the bed, heart jumping as fast as the heart monitor beeped,. It jumped from 96 to 148 to 182 in a few seconds, and raced to 202 before creeping back down. He had "redlined."

"Mr. Archer, are you okay?" The nurse, panicked, rushed to check his pulse. It slowed further.

"Bad dream," he said. "That's all."

She watched the monitor until it was near the average BPM. She smiled as if to say everything was okay, if not for his sake, at least her own.

She prepared to draw Michael's blood.

After snapping on two pairs of latex gloves, she placed the white basket on the bedside table, preparing a syringe to take three blood samples for a workup. She wrapped a blue elastic band around his upper arm, felt around for a vein, plunged the needle into his arm, giving one of those I'm-sorry-but-I-have-to-do-this smiles.

He understood, and in about two minutes, she was done, bidding him good night as she left the room. But Michael realized that he would not have a good night; not as long as she haunted his dreams.

The words that she spoke took him back almost twenty years to his grandparents' home by Lake Truth. It was small, but cozy, the backyard full of oak and pine trees, like those scenes in the movies; it was beautiful and desolate. Beauty and serenity only a teenager could miss.

Isabel.

Isabel Corene.

Isabel.

Nights long ago by the lake. She'd been his high school girlfriend in 1990. He'd completely forgotten those days—age will do that—life sneaks up, and in the words of his late grandfather, "You need to stick with it before it bites you in the ass."

Why has she come back?

* * *

Four hours passed, and the same nurse came in, did her routine: gloves, syringe, blood, small talk. It was the wee hours of the morning. Michael watched the nurse leave, her soft-soled shoes a whisper on the shiny, antiseptic floor. The door to his room crept closed, the light from the hallway a momentary slice of invasion of the darkness. The door eased shut, plunging the room into a stifling darkness. Michael clamped his eyes closed against the dark, but an overwhelming fear pried them open.

Isabel formed out of the darkness as though her visage fed from its deep nothing.

"You remember me?" she said, her voice ghostly, skin transparent. Michael could see the darkness swirling through her, behind her. She seemed to shimmer from within, skeleton. musculature, veins, and arteries translucent.

"I do," Michael said, sitting up in bed.

"You want to be with me?"

"Isabel-- No. It's been twenty years. You're dead."

She looked away.

"I know what happened," Michael said. "I remember everything."

She looked at him; tears running down her face.

"I remember now," Michael reiterated. "Summer '98, was it? Eight years after us. That's when you died."

She blinked away more tears. They fell to the floor, little slivers of ice..

"I remember reading about it in the paper."

"You were there, at the funeral." She stepped closer.

"Yes." He wanted to run, scream, but realized that somehow she needed this.

She paced alongside the bed, humming a tune, her hair losing its golden shine, her skin no longer glowing, her eyes becoming dark as coal. The murky pits opened and closed like a sleeper waking from a coma, realizing that time had continued to tick away while the sleeper slept. And while the world kept changing, the sun rising and falling, seasons chainging, so too did this sleeper change as a different thing replaced what she once was. The dissatisfaction of early demise always worked this way. The sleeper, blissfully unaware, awakens when anger and the inequitable injustice of sudden death strikes like the palm of God upon the earth.

"They never found who hurt you," Michael said. "Or if anyone did. I remember, now. Some said you killed yourself, drowned in Lake Truth, pockets full of stones."

Her lips curled, her brow furrowed, and her eyes, now caked

with frozen tears of blood, reflected the soulless entity that had awakened Isabel Corene.

"What does it matter?" the thing screamed, its voice screeching like a rusted hinge. "Dead is dead, and when you threw me away…"

It reached for him, grabbing his shoulders, its cold touch chilling him to the bone. Isabel's once dainty hands, now claws of hate and distrust, grasped his throat, squeezing. Michael struggled, trying to speak, resisting, but the thing's strength overpowered his. He thrashed about on the bed. the monitors beeping loudly.

Abruptly, she released his throat, sliding her hands down his chest—into his chest—Isabel's—or the thing she'd become—hands seemed to melt into his chest, through skin and bone, her claw-like grip encircling his heart.

"You murdered me!" the thing screamed, its voice a mixture of Isabel's and a million other murdered young women.

Michael gasped, heart stopped. His muscles relaxed. His eyes shut for the last time.

Now, like her, Michael had a broken heart, too.

Therapy had helped Michael suppress the memory of the awful deed committed a decade ago, but Isabel remembered.

She will always remember.

◇◇◇◇◇

Joseph McGee is a multi-published author of 22 years of age. His short fiction has appeared in various magazines and anthologies, including The Sound of Horror, Winter Frights, Gifts of the Flesh to name a few. His short story, Phil's Place has gained lots of recognition, including a Top Ten spot on the readers' poll for Predators and Editors.

His novels include, In the Wake of the Night, Snow Hill, Dead Winter and the three-story collection, Tripartite (exclusive to Amazon.com's Kindle).

Web site: www.josephmcgee.net.

BEWARE THE BLACK DOG, HARBINGER OF DEATH
KURT BACHARD

"He takes the form of a huge black dog, and prowls along dark lanes and lonesome fields, where, although his howling makes the hearer's blood run cold, his footfalls make no sound ... it is even said that to meet him is to be warned that your death will occur before the end of the year."

This description of a demonic dog, from "Highways & Byways in East Anglia," (1901) is typical of phenomena known generically as Black Dog encounters. Historical and modern archives of the supernatural teem with recorded sightings of these Hellish hounds. The descriptions of these supernatural canines seem to agree: characteristically, they are as large as a calf, with baleful, flaming eyes, twin-headed or even headless, and with an ability to walk on their hind legs, and vanish into thin air. Theo Brown, who made a broad study of the Black Dog between the late 1950s and 1970s, recorded a multitude of local names for the beast and hundreds of sightings throughout parts of Britain, mapping sightings to coastlines, isolated countryside lanes, fields, and secluded funereal spots like churchyards and barrows. In East Anglia, for example, this demonic apparition appears on country lanes to hapless travellers as an omen of death; locals call him "Old Shuck".

Perhaps Old Shuck's basis in the local folklore of Suffolk can be traced back to one of the most widely cited accounts of an early Black Dog encounter. Recorded

> "And if a man shall meet the Black Dog once,
> It shall be for joy,
> And if twice, it shall be for sorrow,
> The third time, he shall die."
> —Old Meriden Proverb. Circa Early 1800s.

by Abraham Fleming in his tract 'A Straunge and Terrible Wunder', Fleming describes his eyewitness account of this supernatural event at a parish church at Bungay, Suffolk, in 1577. During a violent storm, a "black dog, or the divel in such a likenesse ... passed between two persons, as they were kneeling upon their knees...wrung the necks of them bothe at one instant clene backward, in so much that even at a moment where they kneeled, they strangely dyed." The same Black Dog then went on to injure a third to such an extent that "he was presently drawen togither and shrunk up, as it were a peece of lether scorched in a hot fire." The beast then fled to a church at Blythburgh, where it made another assault on parishioners there, slaying two men and a boy. Skeptics have blamed ball lightning; however, the power of the original account diminishes the likelihood that an overlarge black beast could be mistaken for unusual weather occurances.

Modern global sightings of Black Dogs have been comprehensively documented, and paranormal explanations for these supernatural events range from the crude to the sophisticatedly credible. According to some, these apparitions are the wandering spirits of victims of violent deaths, such as the so-called Leandog of Hertfordshire, the black dog spirit seen around the former location of a gallows, or the ghostly dog of Norfolk's tainted Blickling Hall. However, links to funereal locations point to another explanation. The Sussex historian M.A. Lower noted that the path of one particular black dog sighting ran directly from a church to a graveyard along the route of what was once a "coffin road," whereby the dead were conveyed to their burials. Theo Brown's research indicates similar ties with barrows and burial site leylines. In "Mysteries," Colin Wilson also makes this link, as do Janet and Colin Bord in "Alien animals." That black dogs are historically linked to funerary sites is further strengthened by the evidence of the remains of ritually killed dogs found at Neolithic sites of religious significance.

What is in no doubt is that this connection between dogs and the underworld features prominently in almost every ancient religious and mythological text worldwide. The Egyptian God, Anubis, a psychopomp and embalmer, was portrayed as having the head of a black dog, and had links with the Dog Star Sirius, as did the Greek goddess Hecate, another deity occasionally portrayed as dog headed. Designated Guardian of the Underworld, Cerberus, was Hecate's pet, a devilish hound depicted as triple headed, three being a portentously significant number, as we shall see. The Aztec God Xotl, the god of death, also bears the head of a dog. In the Hindu Mahabharata, a dog accompanies Yudhishthira through his tribulations to the gates of heaven. In Norse Mythology, a bloodstained dog called Garm guards the gate at the Land of the Dead. It has also been suggested that during the Bronze and Iron Age, the role of the dog in burial ceremonies was a distinctly macabre one as ground burials were rare in Europe and the newly dead were cleaned of flesh by means of dogs, the consumption of the body equating the ingestion of the spirit.

All this may well go some way to corroborating the theory that these night-stalking death omens are re-enacting or serving their ancient roles as guardians of

Castle Craig overlooking Meriden, CT, near where the Black Dog has been seen.

the dead along ancient leylines or corpse ways specifically designed for conveying coffins directly from churches to gravesites. Moreover, writer Baring-Gould suggested that the custom of sacrificing a black dog in a church foundation creates a Church Grim of the animal, sparing unfortunate human souls the eternal duty of otherworldly guardianship, an idea perhaps inspired by the ancient belief that the first person buried in a graveyard acquired the unwanted duty of guarding all those buried thereafter.

The most famous Black Dog tale, however, is not a recorded encounter, but fiction. Arthur Conan Doyle's most famous work, "The Hound of The Baskervilles," (1902) was reputedly based on legends of demonic Black Dogs haunting the Norfolk countryside. Journalist Bertram Robinson recounted the local tale of the devilish hounds that haunted Cromer Hall to Doyle during the latter's convalescent stay at the Royal Links Hotel in Cromer, Norfolk, in 1901. Doyle changed the setting to Dartmoor and the name of the Hall to Baskerville.

All this might give the impression that supernatural Black Dog encounters are a curiously British phenomenon, as idiosyncratically British as the wartime stiff upper lip, but this seeming exclusivity to the English countryside could not be further from the truth. One of the most famous and intriguing cases was recorded the geologist W. H. C. Pynchon and took place in the volcanic hills of Meriden, Connecticut, in the late 1800s, at the ominously named "Hanging Hills," which like the elusive street in Lovecraft's "The Music of Erich Zann," is reputedly hard to find. Pynchon wrote of a spectral black dog the colour of "an old black hat that has been soaked in the rain" seen haunting the West

Peak. Pynchon was already aware of the folklore regarding the black dog of Hanging Hills when he wrote, in his account "The Black Dog," published in The Connecticut Quarterly, "Many have seen him once, a few twice - none have ever told of the third meeting."

Pynchon was collecting samples on ridges that he described as the most desolate of all in the West Peak when the dog first appeared to him. Three years later, he returned to Hanging Hills with Herbert Marshall from the US Geological Survey. Marshall, who had already seen the dog twice, openly mocked the legend and dismissed the omen as unbelievable. However, fate punished his bravado with devastating effect. During a light snowfall the next morning at the "deep clefts," a region that Pynchon compared to the "Valley of the Shadow of Death," both men again encountered the black dog with "breath steaming from his jaws," at which point the rock where Marshall stood gave way. According to Pynchon's account, Marshall turned pale, exclaiming, "'I did not believe it before. I believe it now'," before he plummeted to his death, dashed on the rocks below. It was Marshall's third encounter with the dog.

Pynchon may have escaped the same fate as his friend, for in some accounts he never returned to Hanging Hills. In other accounts, he returned to the West Peak to continue the geological survey, having written, "When I am gone this paper may be of interest to those who remain, for, in throwing light on the manner of my death, it will also throw light on the end of the many victims that the old volcanic hills have claimed." Allegedly, he was found dead in almost the exact same spot where Marshall met his death. To this very day, a number of climbers and tourists to Hanging Hills have come a cropper (perished) under strangely similar circumstances, locals attributing their deaths to sightings of the black dog.

"And if a man shall meet the Black Dog once, It shall be for joy, And if twice, it shall be for sorrow, The third time, he shall die."
Old Meriden Proverb. Circa Early 1800s.

Kurt Bachard *lives in South London, UK, where he was raised as a feral child by stray dogs on a council housing estate. His work has appeared in numerous publications in print and online. He also writes under various pseudonyms.*

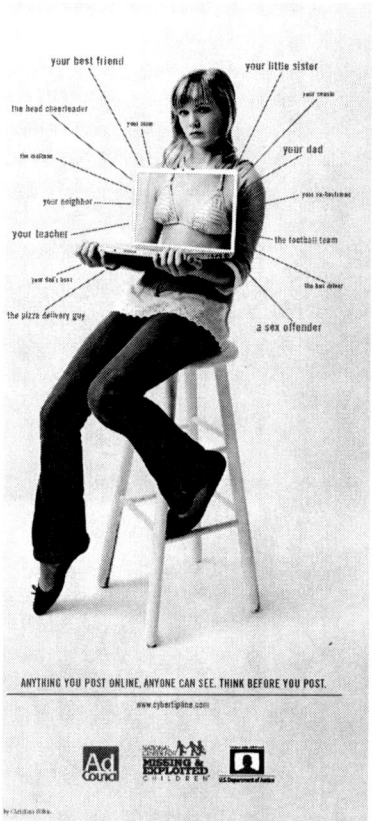

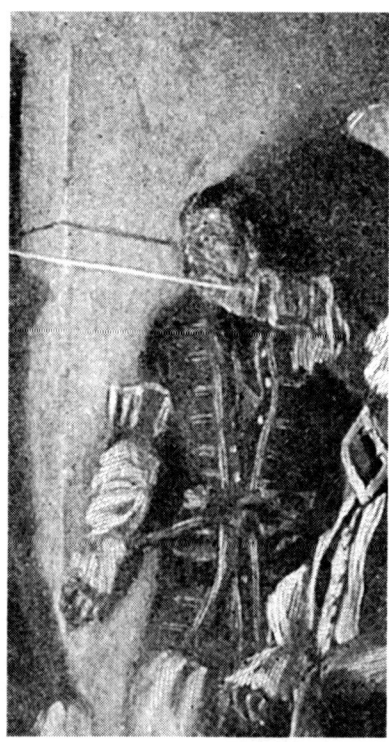

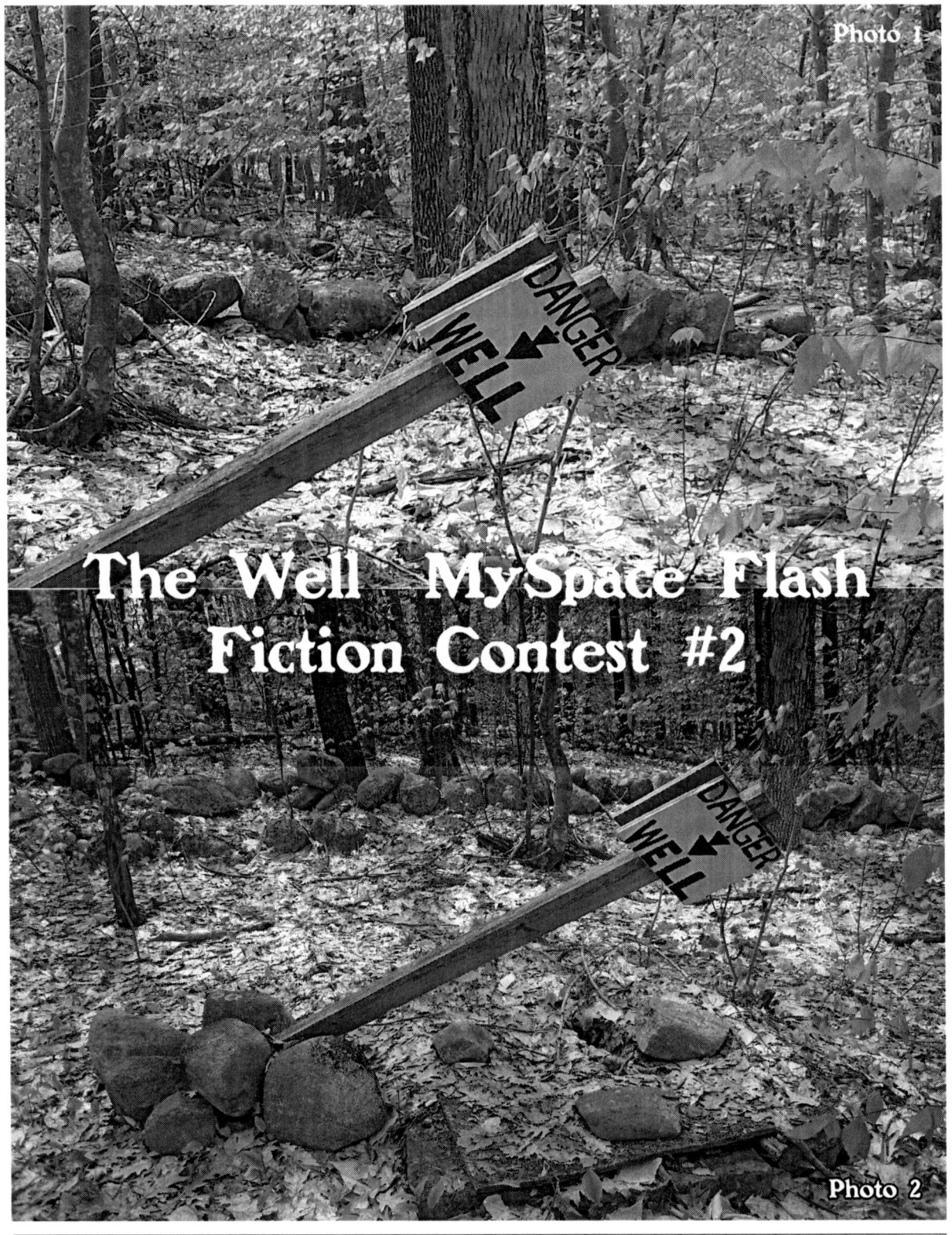

MySpace Flash Fiction Contest #2
"The Well"

It was the first warm and dry day of the spring and it fell on a Saturday, for which I thanked the Gods that be. My mother-in-law had decided to come over and visit with my wife Jenn and work on planting a vegetable garden on our land. I took the opportunity to grab my GPS, some granola bars, and my Camelbak and go geocaching. Geocaching, you ask? It is one of the coolest pastimes I have found. It combines hiking with scavenger hunting. Thousands of participants have hidden caches around the world containing little trinkets and a logbook. You simply go to www.geocaching.com and download the geocoordinates to your GPS and then go hunting. It's a fantastic way to get outside, get some exercise, and explore some places you've never been before. Go ask Mark Rainey, horror author and prolific geocacher. He'll agree, it's both thrilling and satisfying.

It was my first cache of th year and it took me to the peak of Teneriffe Mountain in Milton, NH. I found the cache (after reviewing the clues) in the rotted-out base of a tree. I logged my visit and then took a moment to enjoy the amazing view of Milton Three Ponds, which border West Lebanon, Maine. My route to the cache had taken me down a steep embankment so I decided to find a less "vigorous" route back to my truck. In doing so, I abruptly became lost. Now I had my GPS, and I knew where the geocache was, but like an idiot I had failed to mark my entry point.

Long story short, I found my way to a conservation trail that eventually led back to the road I parked on. But before I reached my truck, I came upon an abandoned well in the woods. It immediately sparked my imagination, and I knew that it would spark our readers' as well. I snapped a few pictures and posted them up on MySpace the first chance I had.

So here we are with the winner and honorable mentions for the 2nd MySpace Flash Fiction contest. Trust me when I tell you there were NO losers, these just stuck out in our mind. We hope to see your entries in the 3rd contest, coming up very soon!

-Tim

Winner:

Title: The Way of All Wishes
Author: William H. Wandless
MySpace ID: William H. Wandless

Lester parked his truck in a clutch of trees near the end of the old logging road. He emptied his trunk, shouldered his load, and strode into the woods. The crowbar he used as a walking stick felt substantial and heavy in his right hand. In comparison, Veronica's body seemed surprisingly light.

Lester clenched his teeth and climbed. Although he had trained for the better part of a year, the burn settled into his muscles sooner than he expected. The incline of the slope was gentle, milder than the flights of stairs he had scaled to prepare, but adrenalin had whetted his senses. Everything seemed brighter and sharper, and his thighs throbbed with every step. He grinned fiercely and pressed onward. Twenty minutes of pain would buy him a lifetime of freedom.

That was the kind of sacrifice that Veronica had never understood. Why scrimp and save when pleasure was there to be purchased? Why go home to the faithful bailiff when she could bed a randy detective? She buzzed like a hummingbird, darting from fix to fix, and Lester had been left to tend the nest. She loved him for his indulgent disposition, and he had once loved her in his staid, deliberate way. Even when she confessed to all her infidelities she thought she could count on steady, sensible Lester. A woman like her could never fathom the depth of his premeditation.

Patience was Lester's cardinal virtue, his way of besting the recklessness of human nature. He had seen too many trials decided by errors made in haste, and he had planned and practiced, reworked and rehearsed. If they bothered to search, his friends on the force would find no signs of struggle; when they hunted for motives, they would turn up one of the many maudlin farewell letters Veronica had written. When a wife goes missing the husband always becomes a suspect, but Lester would be just another clueless fool, the quintessential victim.

All he needed to do was make it to the well. Perched on the northeast face of Mount Teneriffe, far from hiking trails and scenic views, the well had galvanized his resolve. Since he had stumbled upon it he could think of no more perfect proof of his transcendent firmness of purpose than walking that mile and seeing Veronica sink into that water, lost and forever forgotten.

Lester almost dropped to his knees when the well came into view. He staggered forward, slipped his load off his shoulders, and worked his crowbar under the edge of the lid. He levered and lifted, his determination never faltering until it was entirely off, until he knew he was undone, until his hope had yielded completely to horror.

Despite the remote location, despite the enormous effort of the undertaking, Lester was far from the first to be beguiled by the well. It was already full of moldering flesh and broken bones caked in quicklime, its gullet crammed with bodies to the top.

Copyright 2008 William H. Wandless

Runner up

Title: Awakening
Author: R. Scott McCoy
MySpace ID: Necrotic Tissue

Deep in the earth, the dark god Malsum stirs from his long slumber. He searches for his brother, his enemy, Glooskap. The earth still holds the memory of his departure from this plain. Malsum smiles. He senses the Algonquin are also gone, destroyed by the strange pale men with alien minds. They're noisy, scurrying about the land and sky as if by magic. Malsum searches their minds and finds only a few who remember his name.

He is not yet strong enough to venture out. Not yet.

* * *

Greg Travis stares at the blank screen of his GPS unit. He shakes it and swears, but it remains blank. This is his first geocaching adventure and it's not going well. It sounded fun. Someone hides a box with a prize in it and he finds it using his new GPS. At the very least it sounded like good exercise. Now, standing in the middle of New Hampshire's Mount Teneriffe Preserve with a broken GPS unit and no compass, it no longer feels fun.

Greg's overwhelmed with momentary panic and forces himself to breathe. He looks for the sun, but the sky is grey with low hanging clouds. He turns in a circle, hoping for some clue as to what direction to take. A loud whistle comes from his left. He pushes through the underbrush toward the noise and steps into a clearing. A signpost sags in a pile of rocks. The words "Danger, Well", mark a hazard buried beneath a blanket of decayed leaves.

He walks over and kneels down to examine a hole in the wood cover. As he kneels, he realizes he's in the center of a large stone circle. It's not a foundation. Is it circle meant to keep something out, or in?

Pain explodes in his right hand and he falls backwards trying to pull away from whatever's hurting him. There are two small holes leaking milky fluid and only then, does he hear the rattle. He sags to the ground unable to keep his eyes open.

***

Greg wakes in darkness, his arm on fire. He tries to sit up but his legs won't cooperate. A low growl rises from the well. Greg tries to pull himself away with his left arm. Wood and earth explodes behind him and a large stone strikes his back. A huge shape lands only feet in front of him. It's the size of a horse, but is shaped like a dog. No not a dog, a wolf, pitch black with molten eyes. It's mouth hangs open, dripping acid past teeth the size of butcher knives.

Worship me.

The images form in Greg's mind as the thing growls at him.

With great effort, he speaks. "I…I worship you."

The beast steps forward, it's muzzle contorted in a grotesque smile. Malsum, dark god of the true people rips the head from the pale human and swallows it whole. The taste is not unpleasant.

With Glooskap gone, the world is his to ravage.

Copyright 2008 R. Scott McCoy

Runner up

Title: The Worst Sin
Author: Michelle Muenzler
MySpace ID: Drachin8

Leaves crackled like broken glass beneath Mike's boots.

"Damn," he said, covering his ears. "What the hell you got in that well this time?"

Kneeling by the well, Jimmy stabbed his pocket knife at the exposure-grayed boards planked across its opening. "Take a guess."

A grunt, hoarse and breathless, muffled its way from within.

"Coon, maybe. Been there a couple of days."

"Nope."

"Badger?"

Jimmy gave Mike a funny look. "That the best you got?"

Another muffled grunt strained into a low squeal.

"Ah, shit," Mike said. Jimmy was such a fuck. "That's one of Connoly's prize porkers, ain't it? He's gonna skin you alive when he finds out."

"Yeah, sure, what the hell. A pig. Ain't Connoly's, though."

"Then whose is it?"

Jimmy dug a deep slash into the corner of a plank, pairing it up with two others already worn by the recent rains. "Wild. Caught it ruttin' with Angler Johnson."

A shot of bile spiked up Mike's throat.

"Ain't no worse sin," Jimmy continued, "than fornication with animals."

Mike swallowed until the bile slid back into his stomach like a lump of hot clay. "I thought Angler ran off with your sis' to Trenton last week. Before the rains."

"That's what they say." Jimmy rose and wiped his blade across his jeans. "Rumors gotta start somewhere, though. In fact, heard a rumor just a few days back. 'Bout my sister. Thought I'd ask you about it."

A cold streak clenched Mike's groin. He backed off a step. Behind Jimmy, the muffled grunt started up again. Coon, badger? Hell no. The damn thing sounded human.

"Hey now," Mike fumbled about his pockets for something sharp. "I ain't done nothin' to your sis' she didn't want done. You can ask her." His hands came back empty except for a few scraps of napkin. Phone numbers from the bar last night.

The grunting died again, but a low whimper crawled along the back of Mike's skull.

"I already did," Jimmy said, advancing. "And as I said, ain't no worse sin than fornication with animals."

Copyright 2008 Michelle Muenzler

Runner up

Title: Danger Well
Author: Blue Gilliand
MySpace ID: blugilliand

We called it "Danger Well" because that's what the sign said. A bunch of stupid kids who didn't realize it was a warning, not a name. We thought it was cool because it was deep in the woods – too deep for adults to bother with. We liked the way the sign leaned almost to the ground. We liked the small mound of stones that had been arranged at the base of the sign. We speculated about who put the sign there, who piled up the stones, and, naturally, what might have been sealed up in Danger Well.

When we got old enough to camp out alone, we always did it at Danger Well. We'd build a little fire off to the side and put our sleeping bags as close to the Well as we dared. We teased each other about rolling over in our sleep and plunging into the darkness. We dared each other to jump over the Well, which we all eventually did in great, heart-stopping leaps.

Years went by, and we started bringing girls to Danger Well. We'd tell them the stories we'd made up as kids, stories about giant spiders sleeping on great webs that crisscrossed the inside of the Well; about the madman who hid his piles of bones in its dark throat; about slobbering humanoid creatures and in-bred backwoods cannibals who feasted on human flesh and then escaped down the Well to hide.

None of it was true, of course. Danger Well was just a hole in the ground, granted legendary status by a bunch of kids who found it by accident one day.

Until last year, when Roger took his girl up there, and got to drinking and showing off. He told her how we used to dare each other to jump it. Then he showed her how he used to do it, only this time he was drunk and stumbling, a little heavier and a lot less agile. He landed one foot on solid ground, she said, but the other plunged through the leaves and the old rotten boards, and he pinwheeled down into the darkness.

She said he screamed for a long time.

Now we only go there to leave flowers, and to toast the memory of our friend. We carved "Roger" into the old leaning sign.

It's a warning, not a name.

Copyright 2008 Blu Gilliand

Runner up

Title: Remnants of Innocence Lost
Author: Jason Keene
MySpace ID: keenehorror

Mark sat perched atop the stack of rocks beneath him with his weary head hung low and sullen. The depth of the woods that embraced him always seemed to take on a less somber tone during the light of the day. And yet, the despair still lingered heavy through the silence whether it was accompanied by the shaded rays of day or the silken throws of midnight.

Mark had happened upon the old cabin many years ago during a hunting excursion with his friends as a teenager. They would take refuge in the worn relic as night would close in around them before renewing their efforts the following morning. Sometimes when they couldn't sleep, they would go outside and sit around the well and talk of their futures; college and women and the hopes of moving away from their rural backwoods prison. But the days of youth were long gone, as was the beaten remnants of the old wooden cabin.

He stared out upon the broken frame of the nearby shack. The dark boards lay across each other in melancholy shambles. The evening's waning beams of light filtered through the thick branches of the forest's canopy and left shadowed images across the pile of rubble. Mark sighed as he reflected upon his last night in the cabin.

His best friend, Anthony, had come along with them reluctantly. The five of them had settled in for the evening and fallen asleep. During the night, Mark was roused from his sleep by a rustling outside. He reached cautiously for his rifle on their makeshift bench. The thought of a bear infiltrating their camp sent his nerves into an uproar and he sat listening while the invader scurried about. Mark's trembling hands fumbled about as he slowly inched his way to his feet and stepped cautiously through the dark towards the window. Bathed in the moonlight was a shadowed figure standing alongside the old well. Mark raised his rifle and his pulse quickened. He leaned forward and put his eye against the scope, hoping for a clear shot at the beast. His trembling finger pulsed momentarily against the trigger sending a premature blast into the beast, sending it over into the well as Mark recoiled backwards. The shattered remnants of the window's glass followed him to the ground and he lay still.

Mark touched his neck and sat up, letting his fingers run across the jagged slivers of glass imbedded in his throat. He tossed the wood and stones covering the well to the side and took Anthony's hand, helping him up to the surface. The ragged hole left by the gunshot in Anthony's chest always brought a tear to Mark's eye before his friend would wipe it aside with a sad grin. For years the two boys have reunited and stood above Anthony's deep forgotten grave and talked of days long gone; of chances lost and what their futures may have held.

Copyright 2008 Jason Keene

Runner up

Title: The Horde,
Author: Ginger Nielsen
MySpace ID: Gingër

The boy still held the bird in his hand. It felt slight and weightless, like holding a tissue. It's head was resting on the thick part of Toby's palm. The tiny beak was parted; something thick and pinkish-red oozed from in between, it's dull black eyes were lifeless. A few moments ago the bird had been fluttering madly, trying desperately to escape the boy's hold on it. He watched as it became more panicked as Toby's grip tightened. He felt it's rib cage beneath it's wings, felt it give in and collapse. He knew what he did was wrong, or at least that no one else did these things. He once asked the neighbor boy, Tommy, if he'd ever killed anything. Tommy assumed he meant like hunting. This wasn't hunting though. This was pure and simple killing, with your own bare hands. I ended your life. I made you stop breathing, forever.

Toby grinned at the thought. When he got to the well he removed the stones, then slid the wooden lid off as a few stray flies lazily flew out of the opening. The smell was instant and overwhelming, of decay and death. When he looked down, he saw the black shimmer of remnant water and rot. He could hear the buzz of flies, a continuous drone, and when he listened long enough, the sound changed somehow, it took on kind of a tuneless chant. He never understood what was being said, though on some days he would just lay by the well, listening. The bird barely made a soft splish sound when it hit the bottom, and Toby watched with his hands on his knees, peering down into the well.

"   Tobias Mitchell!" his mother's voice caused him to teeter forward, and for one horrific moment, he reeled over the well, arms waving, then finally catching and straightening himself. He looked at his mother, trying for innocence. "What?"

His mother's face was red, arms crossed tightly over her chest. "I saw you back there, I saw what you did." Her expression took on a sour look. "You've done this before." It wasn't a question. Toby stood defiantly. "So? Their just stupid animals. Dad says they ruin the crops."

"I'm telling your father about this. This isn't right, Toby. You can't-" her breath caught in her throat as she looked past him, at the ground near the well. She walked near Toby, reached down with a shaking hand. She held up the dog's collar, their dog's collar.

"Smokie.." She breathed.

"What is wrong with you!" She hissed. She clutched Smokie's collar, the tags jangled as she thrust her hand out to him. "You need to be put away! How many other animals were there, Toby?" She peered down into the well as the flies buzzed angrily. Toby stepped towards his mother. All he could hear were the flies now, and something else. Toby listened and finally understood. He put his hands on his mothers back, and pushed.

Copyright 2008 Ginger Nielson

Prize

William H. Wandless, our winner, received:

Paid Publication in Issue 3 and a Shroud Prize Bundle that included:

2 Cult Horror DVDs
1 Shroud Anthology
1 Copy of Brian Keene's D*ead Sea.*

Our runners-up received publication. Please visit us on MySpace at www.myspace.com/shroud.

"Look, it's not you, it's me..."

"I just need some space right now..."

"It's just not the right time for a relationship..."

"No, there is not someone else..."

"I just think we'd be better off as friends..."

"Yes, you heard me, let's just be friends..."

www.myspace.com/shroudmag

CAN WE BE FRIENDS?

Shroud 3   The Journal of Dark Fiction and Art

Windows to the Soul
Film and DVD Reviews

Dario Argento's
The Third Mother: The Mother of Tears
Review by Tim Deal

Dario Argento concludes his *Mother of Tears* trilogy with "La Terza Madre," or "The Third Mother: The Mother of Tears," a 2007 Italian/American supernatural horror production that stars his daughter Asia Argento, along with Daria Nicolodi, Moran Atias, Udo Kier, and Coralina Cataldi-Tassoni. Dario Argento produced and directed the film, and shares writing credits with Jace Anderson, Walter Fasano, Adam Gierasch, and Simona Simonetti.

Argento is best known for his influential and violent film *Suspiria,* though he had previously released a number of successful Italian thrillers such as *The Cat o' Nine Tails* (1971) and *Four Flies on Grey Velvet* (1972), and *The Bird with the Crystal Plumage*—frequently referred to as his "animal trilogy". In addition, Argento is well known for collaborating with George Romero on "Dawn of the Dead."

Often referred to as "surreal and visionary," *Suspiria*, a visually stimulating and edgy film, was intended to be the beginning of a trilogy of films about "The Three Mothers." These were three witches existing in three different modern cities.

Argento followed *Suspiria* with *Inferno* in 1980. Unlike Suspiria, Inferno received a very limited theatrical release and the film did not receive the same box-office success of its predecessor. While the initial critical response to the film was mostly poor, its reputation has improved considerably over the last couple of decades.

In *La Terza Madre*, Sarah Mandy (Asia Argento) is an American studying art restoration at the Museum of Ancient Art in Rome. Sarah discovers and examines an urn found at an ancient gravesite near Viterbo. There she finds the relics of a witch known as the "Mother of Tears," Mater Lachrimarum (Moran Atias).

When Sarah breaks the seal, it

Ania Pieroni in Argento's INFERNO

tleties of Argento's work.

This may not be Argento's best work to date, but it is well crafted, entertaining, viscerally powerful, and provokes thoughts so uncomfortable they may border on disturbing.

◇◇◇◇◇◇◇◇◇◇◇◇◇◇◇◇◇◇◇◇◇◇◇◇◇◇◇◇

causes the return of the witch's powers, and the world is subsequently thrust into horror. Thereafter, a crime wave plagues Italy's capital as witches gather to pay homage to their queen. Sarah eventually discovers her own hidden powers with the assistance of her dead mother (Daria Nicolodi) and then confronts Lachrimarum at the Palazzo Varelli.

While the film will certainly generate a strong reaction from critics, *La Terza Madre* represents a refreshing departure from the cookie-cutter Japanese remakes flooding the box office, as well as the torture-porn blood-fests like *Saw, Hostel*, and *Turistas*, that seem to pass as horror in today's film market. Make no mistake about it, La Terza is unforgivably brutal and bloody, but it possesses a vibrant lushness that makes it a spectacle for the eyes. This film will likely polarize fans of Argento because some of the surreal qualities found in Suspiria border on nonsensical in *Madre*—an issue that will likely create contentious camps that argue the philosophical depth of the movie. However, it is important to give each set piece the attention it deserves in order to discover the artistic sub-

Dark Effigies
Artists Within the Genre

The Amazing Art of Bart Willard
Interview by Tim Deal

With a career in art & design that started 13 years ago, Bart has spent the last five years working out of his studio in Warren, Indiana. His humble beginnings as a contract graphic designer and illustrator have grown, over the years, into the sci-fi, fantasy, and horror art he enjoys working on these days.

Combining his Christian faith with the fact that he is a sci-fi, fantasy, and horror junkie (yes, a Christian can enjoy a good horror story Bart asserts) has produced what he believes to be a unique style and personal aesthetic. "I'm definitely not your garden variety Christian artist, and I'm quite willing to address subjects and themes in an unconventional way," said Willard, "I enjoy using symbolism, metaphor and my personal brand of imagery to get the point across in stark and sometimes unsettling ways."

Bart Willard's art has been used for book & magazine covers, CD album covers, game art and he has even created a few murals.

Bart is this issue's cover artist.

Q&A

Tim Deal [TD] Who are some of your influences?

Bart Willard [BW] Brom, Frank Frazzeta, Boris Valejo, Simon Bizley

[TD] What kind of art were you creating in your 7th grade art class?

[BW] That's a long time ago but I'll try to remember. It seems like we did a lot of two- and three-point perspective and some life drawing. I did a portrait of my dad from a photo of him in his Air Force uniform and we had to do a drawing of our hand. One guy in the class got a little disgusted with me because I had done such a good job on mine. I liked to do lots of Star Wars and other sci-fi stuff on my own time.

[TD] What was and is your preferred media?

[BW] Digital media is my favorite. I enjoy painting, but I'm impatient. It takes too long and I don't like to clean up the mess afterwards. Digital is quick and clean. I also like to work in pencil and I like cartooning.

[TD] Favorite 1980s teen comedy?

[BW] Ferris Bueller's Day Off

[TD] Favorite 1970s horror flick?

[BW] Alien

[TD] Name three things that absolutely terrify you.

[BW] 1. Heights - being on a high place with a small foothold with nothing secure to hold on to pretty much paralyzes me. The scene in The Matrix where Neo had to climb out the window and try to get to the scaffold made me gasp.

2. Large insects - Camel spiders and large insects like the kind you find in a rain-forest creep me out. Not so much terror - I just don't like them - they seem unnatural.

3. To this day I don't know why this is because the movie didn't really terrify me, but the dead mother from The Grudge stuck with me when I first saw it. I couldn't get to sleep that night because I kept seeing her face. Again - her overall appearance was just unnatural, and it unnerved me.

[TD] Can you give us the evolution of your current technique?

[BW] I've never been able to really decide if I'm a sculptor who likes to illustrate or an illustrator who likes to sculpt, but my technique developed out my love for both. As the technology evolved to do 3-D and digital illustration, so did my technique. There are so many tools at the artist's disposal now, and being the technophile that I am, but still loving some of the more traditional mediums and techniques, I've developed a bit of a hybrid system to create my art. As a kid, I loved to build stuff (and still do), but I also loved to draw, and I think it was just natural for me to be drawn to 3-D modeling. I can, in a virtual sense, both sculpt and paint in the same piece. Three-dimensional modeling is a great way to create the foundation of my illustrations, but it can be very time consuming to try to do things in 3-D to keep the art from looking stale and plastic. There are things, from an illustrator's standpoint, that are much, much quicker and easier to do in Photoshop that give the illustrations the character and atmosphere needed. It's very hard for me to create the mood of the piece in 3-D. I guess it's a little bit like Victor Frankenstein creating his creature. He put all of the pieces together but had nothing more than a patchwork corpse on his table. His creation wasn't finished until he put life into it. My work looks pretty stale, lifeless, and unfinished as pure 3-D, but some really exciting things start to happen when I switch into painter/illustrator mode to finish the piece.

[TD] Where do you find your subjects?

[BW] Mostly books and movies. My Christian faith also has a very real influence on the subjects that I choose, and how I try to communicate certain themes. (A Christian who loves horror? Go figure. Yea... we're not all fans of the Pat Robertson version of Christianity.) Ancient history and mythology is also an interest of mine from which I draw a lot of inspiration.

[TD] Tell us two things no one knows about you...

[BW] That's hard because I have friends and loved one's that know almost everything about me but...

1. Not many know that I accidentally shot my cousin in the chest with a bb gun when I was about 12. He survived and was kind enough not to tell our grandpa, who owned the gun and told us not to play with it.

2. I had my first kiss from a girl when I was 5 years old. She kissed me on the cheek, not on the lips.

[TD] Where can we expect to see your work in 2008? What direction are you planning to take your art?

[BW] Right now, I have several irons in the fire. I'm taking much of what I do and starting up a creative agency/studio that serves the haunted house and dark attractions industries as well as putting some energy into a part of my studio that will focus on Steampunk style props, art, and artifacts (ooo... steampunk horror, I need to try that!) I'm also working with a small startup video game studio developing games for (hopefully) the PS3. I can't say much more, but hopefully, something more will happen with that in the near future.

You can learn more about Bart Willard at www.bartwillard.com.

Shroud 3   The Journal of Dark Fiction and Art

***

Who is HIRAM GRANGE?

www.hiramgrange.com

Coming soon...

***

Shroud 3   The Journal of Dark Fiction and Art

Puzzled
by I.E. Lester
Horror Novel Titles

Across

1	Stephen King - Dog -

	1981 (4)
7	see 21 down
8	See 16 down
10	Ray Garton - Were-

	wolves - 2008 (8)
11	See 28 across
12	See 55 across
15	Thomas M. Disch - Med-

Shroud 3   The Journal of Dark Fiction and Art

ical Doctor - 1989
The _. _. (1,1)
17   David Seltzer - Possession - 1976
The ____ (4)
18   Stephen King - Clown - 1986 (2)
20   Mark Chadbourn - Immortal being - 1996
The _____ (7)
22   (50 down) Stephen Gallagher - Boxing - 2007
The _____ of _____ (7, 5)
23   See 21 down
25   See 32 down
28   (with 11 across) Stephenie Meyer - Vampires - 2008 (8, 4)
29   See 47 down
34   (with 35 across) Brian Keene - Zombies - 2007 (4, 3)
35   See 34 across
36   See 56 across
37   (with 8 down) Kathe Koja - Head Injury / Visions - 1992 (3, 6)
40   (with 41 down) Guy Burt - Being Trapped - 1993
After ___ ____ (3, 4)
42   See 32 down
43   Jack Ketchum - Animal Cruelty - 1995 (3)
44   (with 19 down) Laurell J. Hamilton - "Anita Blake" - 2008 (5, 4)
46   (with 40 down and 27 down) Dean Koontz - Madman - 1985
The ____ __ _____ (4, 2, 8)
51   Robert R. McCammon - Demon - 1978 (4)
52   (with 26 down) L.H. Maynard & M.P.N. Sims - Weekend Dinner Party - 2007 (5, 4)
55   (with 12 across) Thomas Tessier - Psychic Powers - 1997 (3, 5)
56   (with 36 across) Stephen King - Death Row - 1996
The ____ ____ (5, 4)
57   Mary Shelley - Artificial Man - 1818 (12)
58   (with 45 down) Simon Clark - place, Skelbrooke, Yorkshire - 2001

Down

2   Peter Benchley - Shark - 1974
3   See 21 down
4   Mark Morris - Flood - 2007
The _____ (6)
5   See 48 down
6   Douglas Clegg - Possession - 2006 (4)
7   See 16 down
8   See 37 across
9   See 16 down
11   Stephen King - Paintings - 2008 (4, 3)
13   See 47 down
14   See 48 down
16   (with 7 down, 9 down and 8 across) Harry Shannon - place, Two Trees, Nevada - 2002 (5, 2, 3, 5)
19   See 44 across
21   (with 3 down, 7 across and 23 across) John Saul - place, St. Albans, Louisiana - 1999
The ____ ____ __ ____ (5, 4, 2, 4)
23   (with 24 down) Anthony Izzo - place, New York City - 2007 (4, 7)
24   See 23 down
26   See 52 across
27   See 46 across
28   P.C. & Kristin Cast - Vampires - 2007
The _____ (8)
30   See 53 down
31   See 53 down
32   (with 42 across and 25 across) V.C. Andrews - place, Foxworth Hall - 1983 (5, 2, 9)
33   See 52 down
38   Douglas Clegg - Private School - 2000 (8)
39   Michael Grant - Disappearances - 2008 (4)
40   See 46 across
41   See 40 across
45   See 58 across
47   (with and 13 down) E.E. Knight - Vampires - 2001
___ of ___ ____ (3, 4)
48   (with 5 down and 14 down) Jonathan Maberry - place, Pine Deep, Pennsylvania - 2008 (3, 4, 6)
49   See 53 down
50   See 22 across
51   Barb Hendee - Vampires - 1999
_____ Memories (5)
52   (with 33 down) Brian Keene - Satyr - 2008 (4, 6)
53   See 54 down
54   (with 53 down, 31 down, 49 down and 30 down) Ramsey Campbell - Silent Movie Star - 2008
___ ____ __ __ ____ (3, 4, 2, 3, 4)

Answers on next page.

The Solution (No Peeking)

Shroud 3   The Journal of Dark Fiction and Art

Shroud Submission Guidelines

Fiction: Shroud considers horror, dark mystery, dark fantasy and suspense short stories up to 5,000 words. In addition, we are interested in tightly woven flash fiction, and (in some cases) serialized novellas. Thriller and Suspense tales with a horror aspect are also welcome. We HIGHLY recommend that you buy a SAMPLE ISSUE in order to get a clear idea of our style and tone.

We are especially interested in:

Mythic horror in a real world setting; Classically-themed horror and suspense; Supernatural horror; Creature horror; Dark Fantasy in a contemporary/RW setting; Noir with a horror element.

We are LESS interested in:

Hard Science Fiction; Sword and Sorcery or anything set in a fantasy world; Stories about serial killers; Vampires ala Rice; First person accounts.

Submission Format: Send us electronic submissions in .DOC or .RTF format as a file attachment. Your subject line should clearly say "SUBMISSION". Simultaneous submissions are NOT okay. Please do not send us multiple submissions -- please only send us one story at a time and do not send your next submission until we give you a reply to the first. Reprints are fine provided they have not been published within three months and the author currently bears the copyright. A short bio would be nice, including any awards or published credits, however your story will stand on its own merit.

Response Time: Averages 2 to 4 months, but stories kept for further consideration by the editors may take additional time.

IMPORTANT: If you have NOT received an acknowledgment of receipt for your SHORT STORY within 1-5 Days of your submission then it is likely the submission was formatted incorrectly. We do appreciate your hard efforts and your creative vision, but with more than 350 submissions a month, if your submission is incorrectly formatted then it will be (unfortunately) deleted... sorry.

Artwork: Please query with samples. We are actively looking for talented artists for covers and B&W interior illustrations.

Nonfiction: Looking for well-researched stories on supernatural phenomenon, dark music, art, and interviews of key players within the genre, film reviews, game reviews. Query first. Payment .02-.03 cents a word.

Payment: Rates of .02 (most) to .05 (very few) cents per word, plus one contributor copy. Payable within 30 days of publication. Up to 5,000 words; maximum payment of $250. All rights revert to the author upon publication.

Anthologies: We automatically consider all fiction submissions for our active anthologies. If accepted, Shroud pays .01 cents a word plus two copies of the published collection.

Send To: editor@shroudmagazine.com

Novels and Novellas

Submission Guidelines (continued)

Shroud publishing is interested in building a catalog of intelligent dark fiction novels and novellas. If you have a COMPLETED manuscript or a series of short fiction, please query with a short synopsis and one sample chapter. Send to the editor.

A note on novel and novella submissions: we are a small press. We have a small press budget. If we are able to put your novel or novella into print we will do our best to market and distribute it, but the likelihood of you or us getting rich is very slim. Consider long and hard before you submit to us. We do not offer advances and our royalty rates will be modest. Having said that, if accepted, we will edit, design, layout your book, get it printed, sell it direct, and do our very best to get it distributed through a major distributor. WE will incur all of the aforementioned expenses, not you. We will never charge you for reading or publishing your book. Nor should you ever be.

So if this works for you, we'd love to see your novel/novella.

Response time for novels/novellas could be 3-6 months as our reading time permits.

***

For more information about Shroud please vist our Website at:

WWW.SHROUDMAGAZINE.COM

See our publications, join our forums, send suggestions, and more.

***

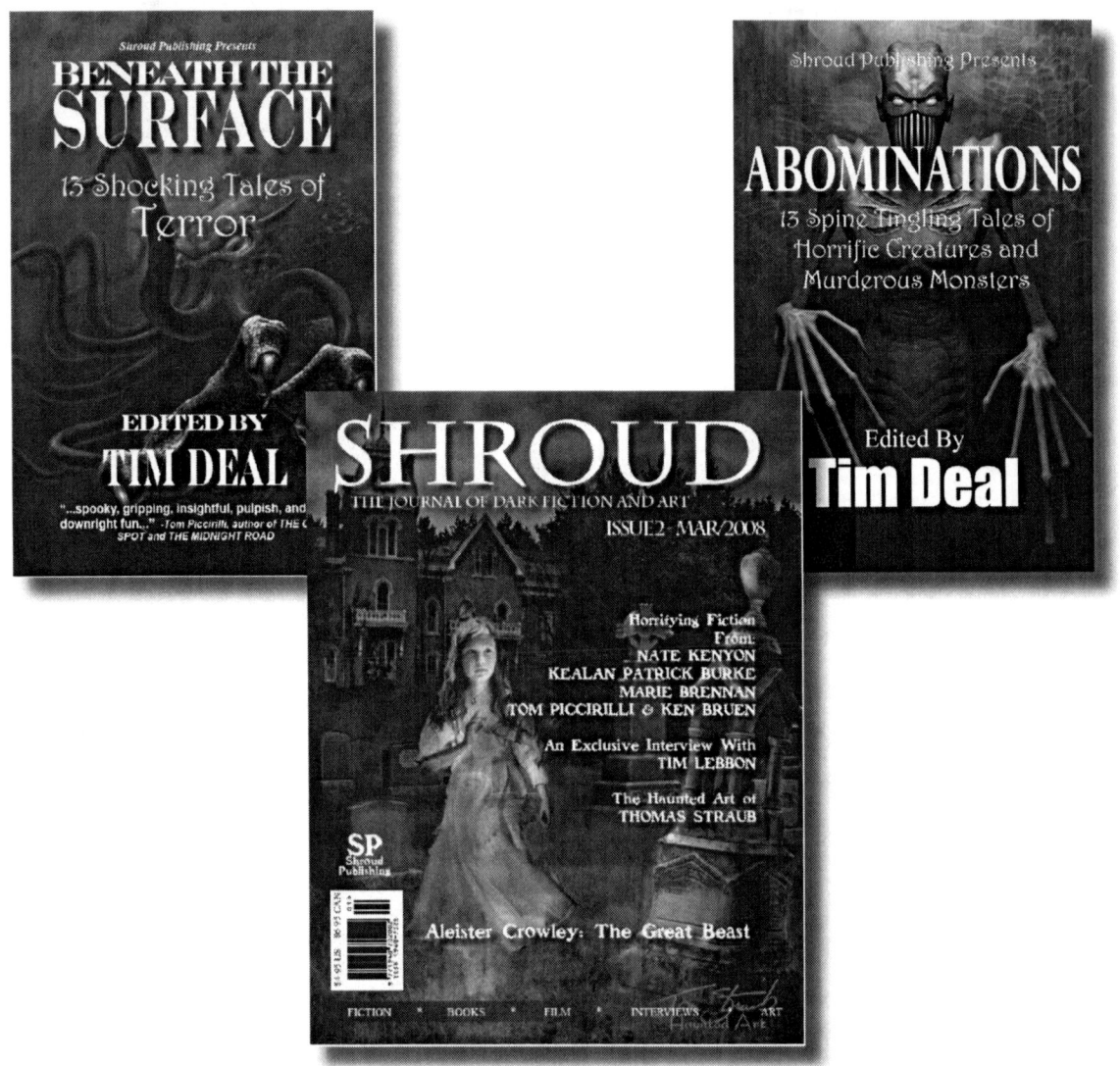

Indulge Your Dark Appetites...

Grab Your Favorite Blanky and Light a Fire.
Get Lost in a World of
MYSTERY, SUSPENSE, AND HORROR

Order today
at
WWW.SHROUDMAGAZINE.COM

Made in the USA